BATMAN
THE BRAVE AND THE BOLD®

STONE ARCH BOOKS
a capstone imprint

STONE ARCH BOOKS™
Published in 2013
A Capstone Imprint
1710 Roe Crest Drive
North Mankato, MN 56003
www.capstonepub.com

Originally published by DC Comics in the U.S. in single magazine form as Batman: The Brave and the Bold #6.

Cataloging-in-Publication Data is available at the Library of Congress website:
ISBN: 978-1-4342-4706-3 (library binding)

Summary: Batman is up against a man with all the time in the world...General Immortus! And only one hero can back Batman up by summoning help from across the ages...Kid Eternity!!

STONE ARCH BOOKS
Ashley C. Andersen Zantop *Publisher*
Michael Dahl *Editorial Director*
Donald Lemke & Sean Tulien *Editors*
Heather Kindseth *Creative Director*
Hilary Wacholz *Designer*
Kathy McColley *Production Specialist*

DC COMICS
Rachel Gluckstern & Michael Siglain *Original U.S. Editors*
Harvey Richards *U.S. Assistant Editor*

Printed in China by Nordica.
1012/CA21201277
092012 006935NORDS13

DC Comics
1700 Broadway, New York, NY 10019
A Warner Bros. Entertainment Company

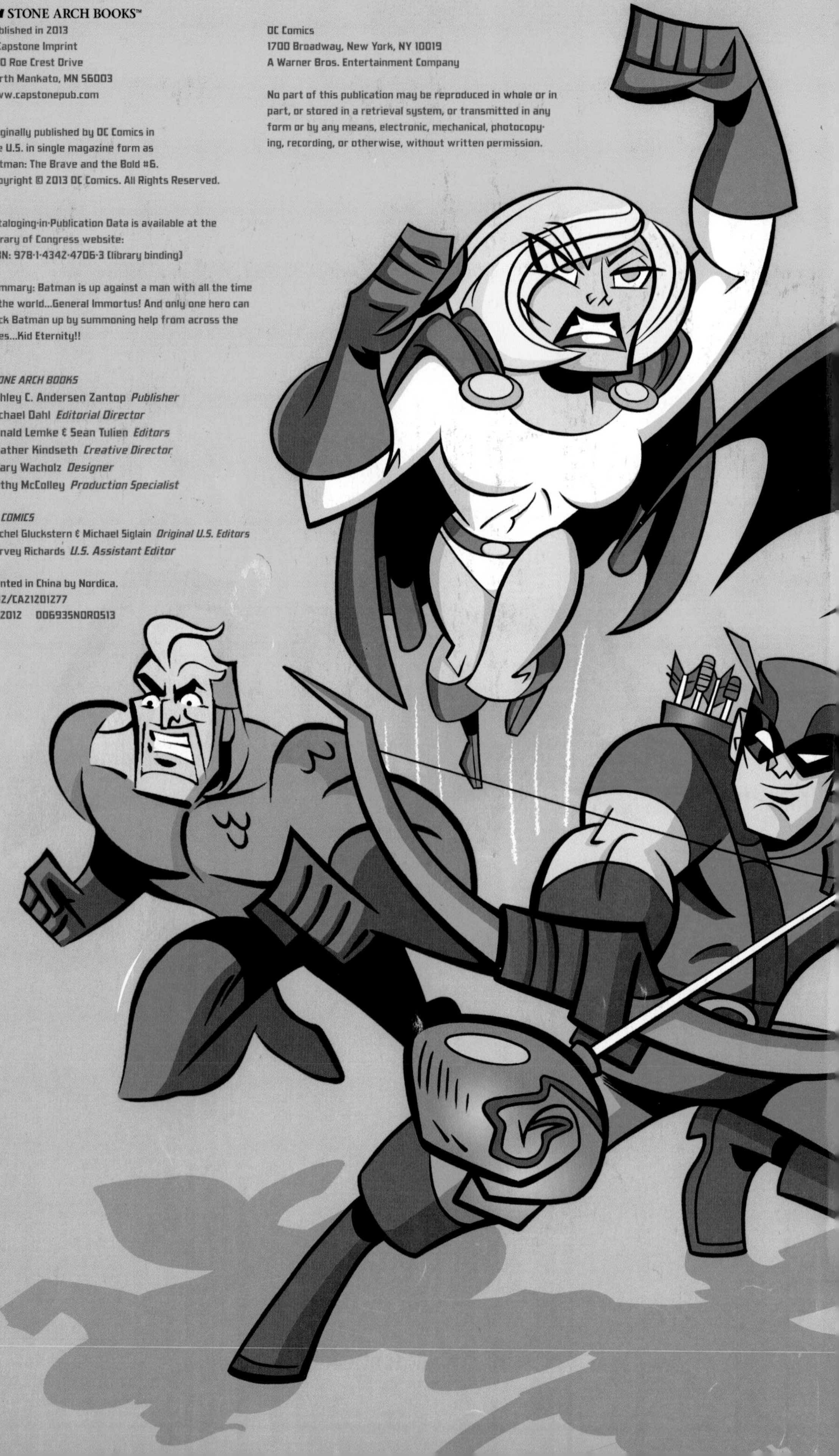

BATMAN
THE BRAVE AND THE BOLD®

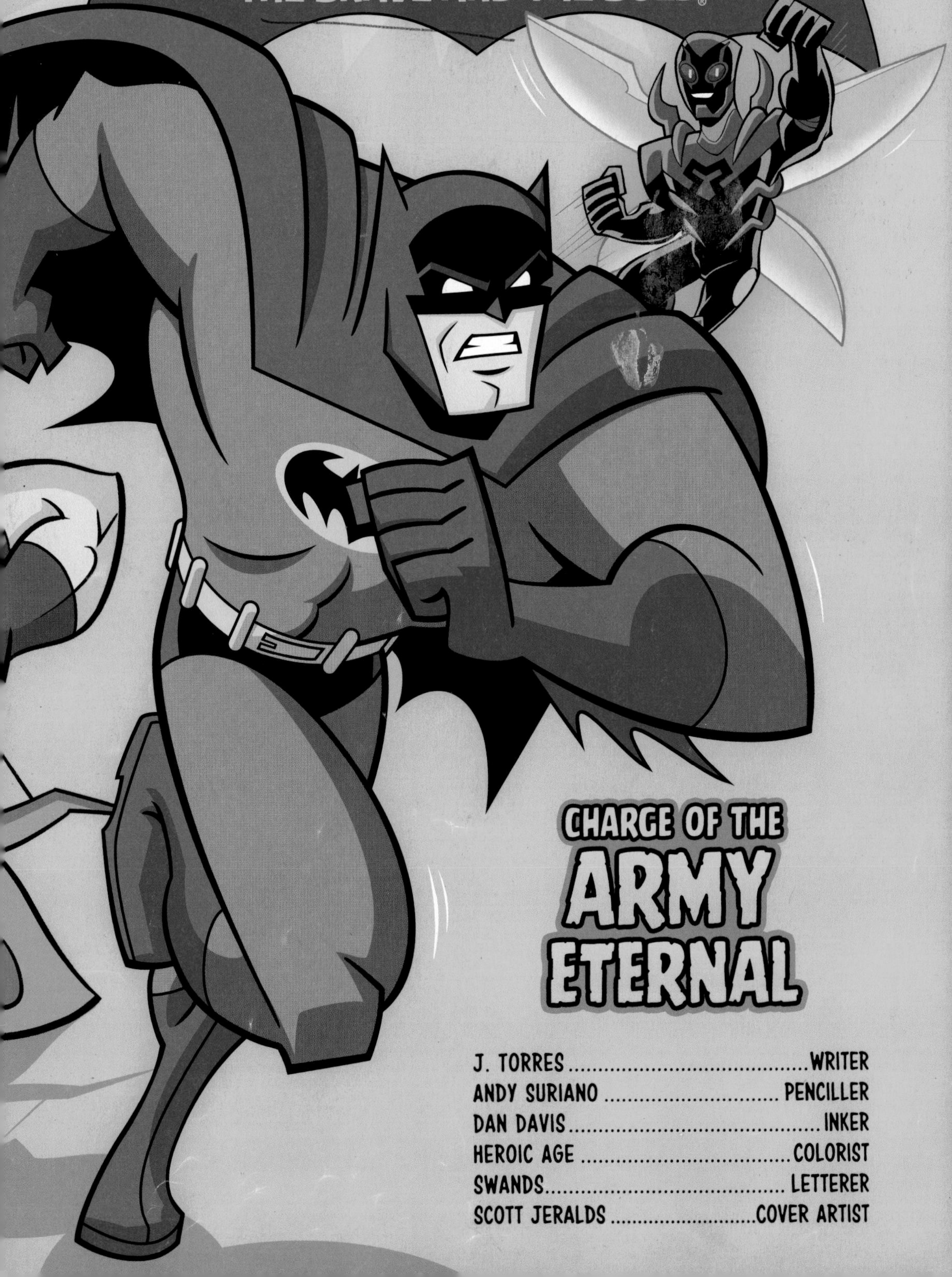

CHARGE OF THE ARMY ETERNAL

J. TORRES..WRITER
ANDY SURIANO .... PENCILLER
DAN DAVIS..INKER
HEROIC AGE ....COLORIST
SWANDS..LETTERER
SCOTT JERALDS ....COVER ARTIST

TIK TIK TIK
BY MY CALCULATIONS, THE EFFECTS OF YOUR "MIRACLO" PILL ARE ABOUT TO WEAR OFF, LEAVING YOU POWERLESS, HOURMAN!
I'D SAY I HAVE AT LEAST ONE MINUTE OF SUPER STRENGTH AND SPEED LEFT TO CLEAN YOUR CLOCK, CALCULATOR!
BUT YOU'RE NOT ONLY OUT OF TIME, YOU'RE OUTNUMBERED AS WELL.
THEN LET'S EVEN THESE ODDS!
MY FOOT PLUS YOUR FACE EQUALS LIGHTS OUT!
POW

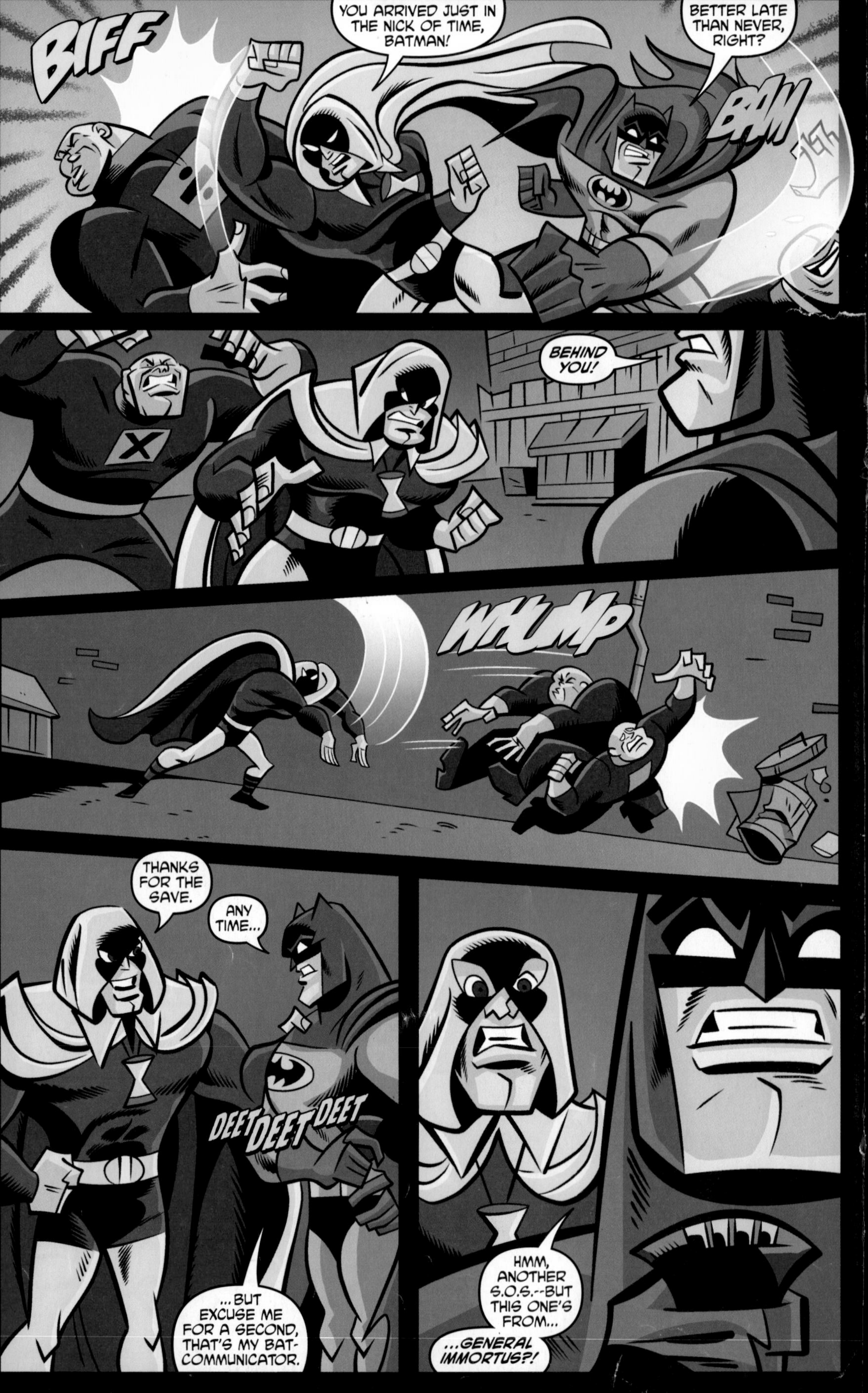
BIFF
YOU ARRIVED JUST IN THE NICK OF TIME, BATMAN!
BETTER LATE THAN NEVER, RIGHT?
BAM
BEHIND YOU!
WHUMP
THANKS FOR THE SAVE.
ANY TIME...
DEET DEET DEET
...BUT EXCUSE ME FOR A SECOND, THAT'S MY BAT-COMMUNICATOR.
HMM, ANOTHER S.O.S.--BUT THIS ONE'S FROM...
...GENERAL IMMORTUS?!

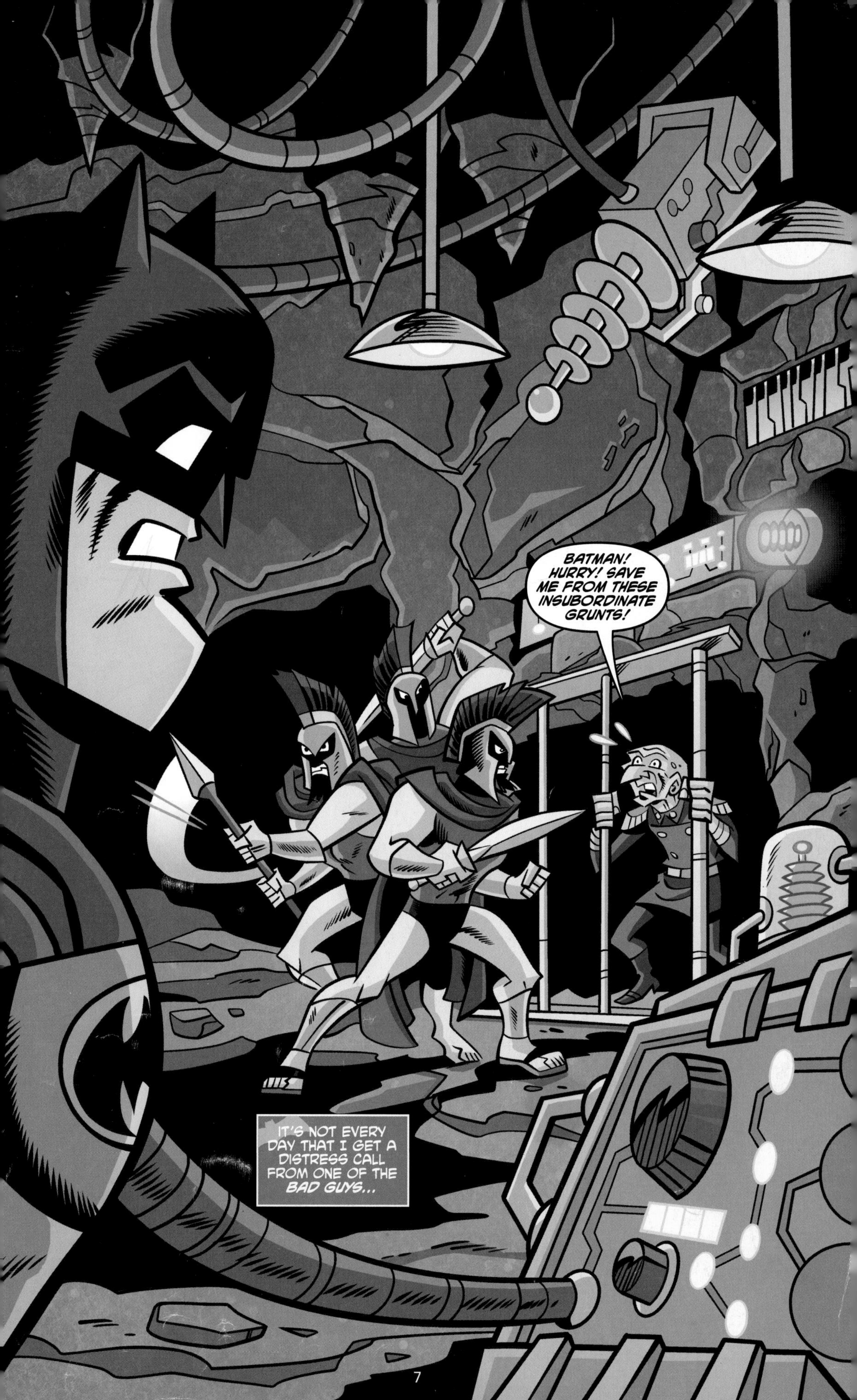
BATMAN! HURRY! SAVE ME FROM THESE INSUBORDINATE GRUNTS!
IT'S NOT EVERY DAY THAT I GET A DISTRESS CALL FROM ONE OF THE BAD GUYS...

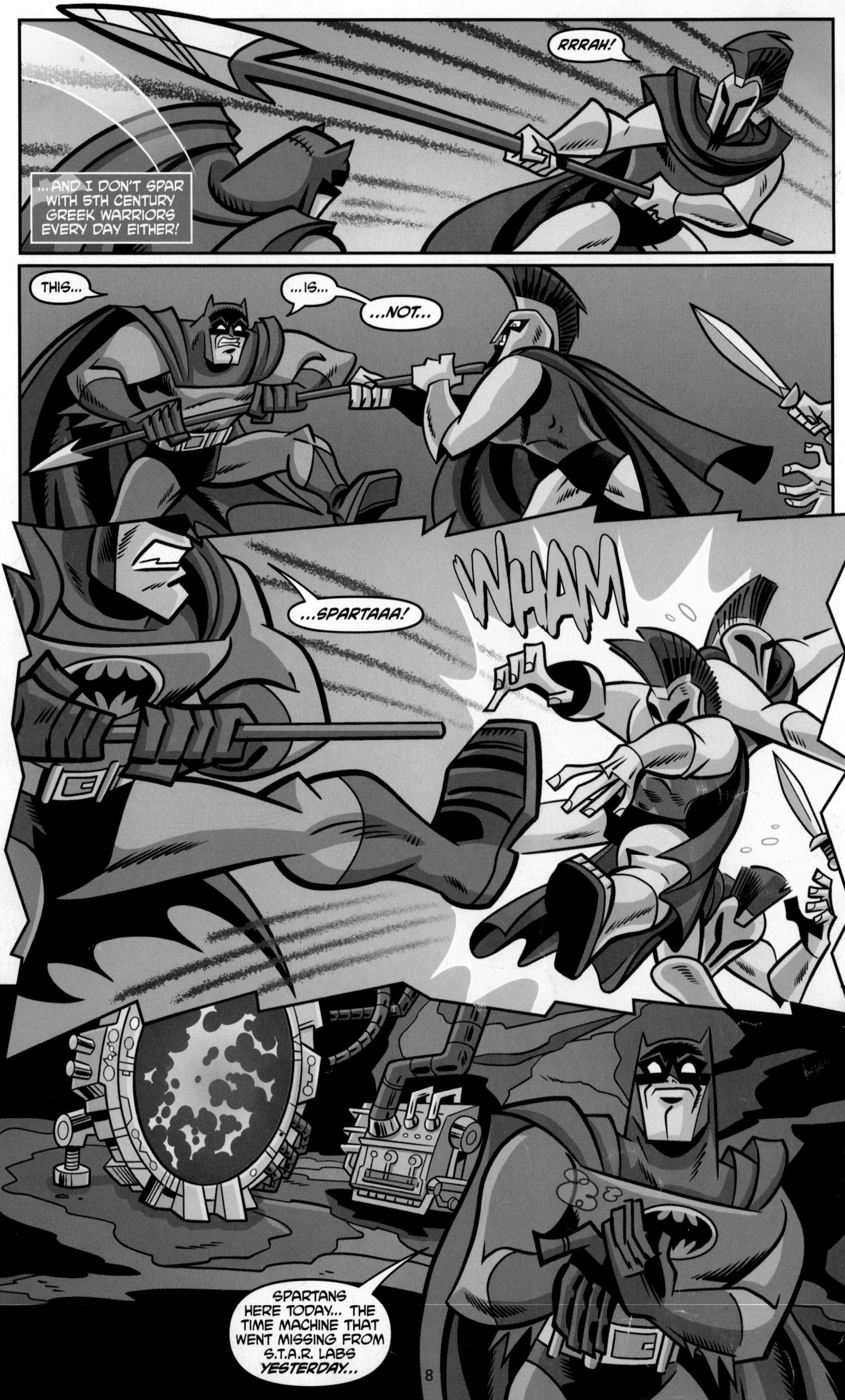
...AND I DON'T SPAR WITH 5TH CENTURY GREEK WARRIORS EVERY DAY EITHER!
RRRAH!
THIS...
...IS...
...NOT...
...SPARTAAA!
WHAM
SPARTANS HERE TODAY... THE TIME MACHINE THAT WENT MISSING FROM S.T.A.R. LABS YESTERDAY...

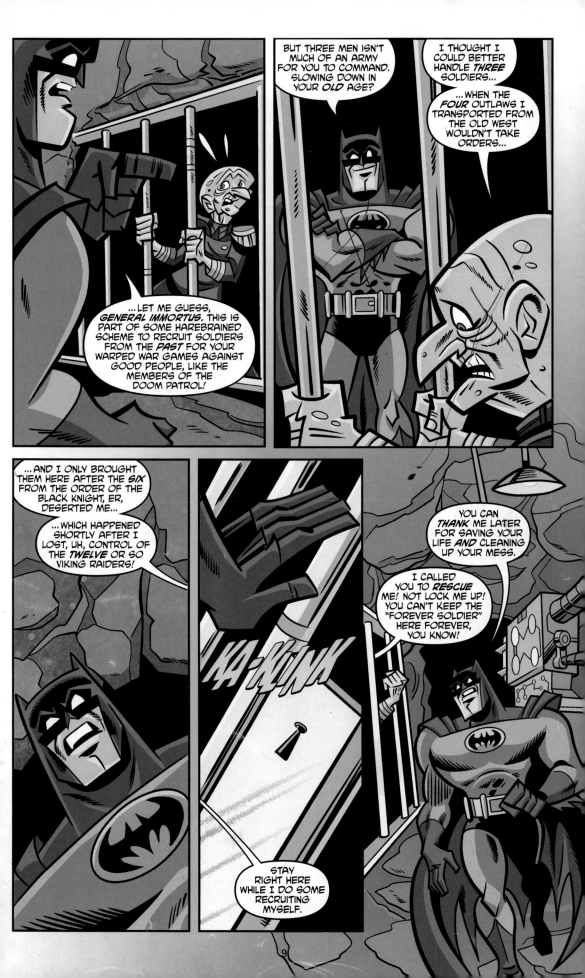

BUT THREE MEN ISN'T MUCH OF AN ARMY FOR YOU TO COMMAND. SLOWING DOWN IN YOUR *OLD* AGE?

I THOUGHT I COULD BETTER HANDLE *THREE* SOLDIERS...

...WHEN THE *FOUR* OUTLAWS I TRANSPORTED FROM THE OLD WEST WOULDN'T TAKE ORDERS...

...LET ME GUESS, *GENERAL IMMORTUS.* THIS IS PART OF SOME HAREBRAINED SCHEME TO RECRUIT SOLDIERS FROM THE *PAST* FOR YOUR WARPED WAR GAMES AGAINST GOOD PEOPLE, LIKE THE MEMBERS OF THE DOOM PATROL!

...AND I ONLY BROUGHT THEM HERE AFTER THE *SIX* FROM THE ORDER OF THE BLACK KNIGHT, ER, DESERTED ME...

...WHICH HAPPENED SHORTLY AFTER I LOST, UH, CONTROL OF THE *TWELVE* OR SO VIKING RAIDERS!

KA-KLUNK

YOU CAN *THANK* ME LATER FOR SAVING YOUR LIFE *AND* CLEANING UP YOUR MESS.

I CALLED YOU TO *RESCUE* ME! NOT LOCK ME UP! YOU CAN'T KEEP THE "FOREVER SOLDIER" HERE FOREVER, YOU KNOW!

STAY RIGHT HERE WHILE I DO SOME RECRUITING MYSELF.

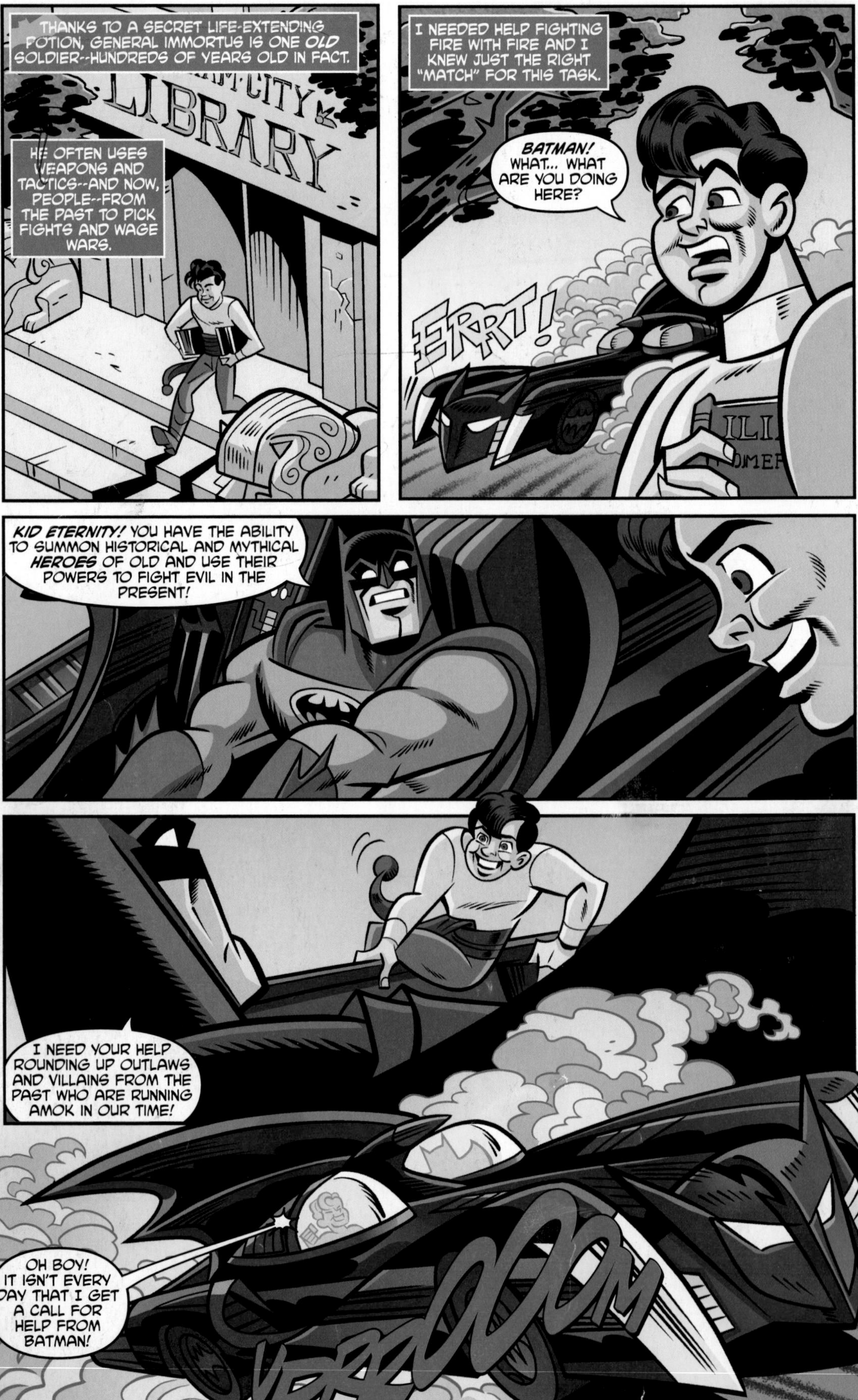

THANKS TO A SECRET LIFE-EXTENDING POTION, GENERAL IMMORTUS IS ONE *OLD* SOLDIER--HUNDREDS OF YEARS OLD IN FACT.
LIBRARY
HE OFTEN USES WEAPONS AND TACTICS--AND NOW, PEOPLE--FROM THE PAST TO PICK FIGHTS AND WAGE WARS.
I NEEDED HELP FIGHTING FIRE WITH FIRE AND I KNEW JUST THE RIGHT "MATCH" FOR THIS TASK.
BATMAN! WHAT... WHAT ARE YOU DOING HERE?
ERRT!
KID ETERNITY! YOU HAVE THE ABILITY TO SUMMON HISTORICAL AND MYTHICAL *HEROES* OF OLD AND USE THEIR POWERS TO FIGHT EVIL IN THE PRESENT!
I NEED YOUR HELP ROUNDING UP OUTLAWS AND VILLAINS FROM THE PAST WHO ARE RUNNING AMOK IN OUR TIME!
OH BOY! IT ISN'T EVERY DAY THAT I GET A CALL FOR HELP FROM BATMAN!
VRRROOOOM

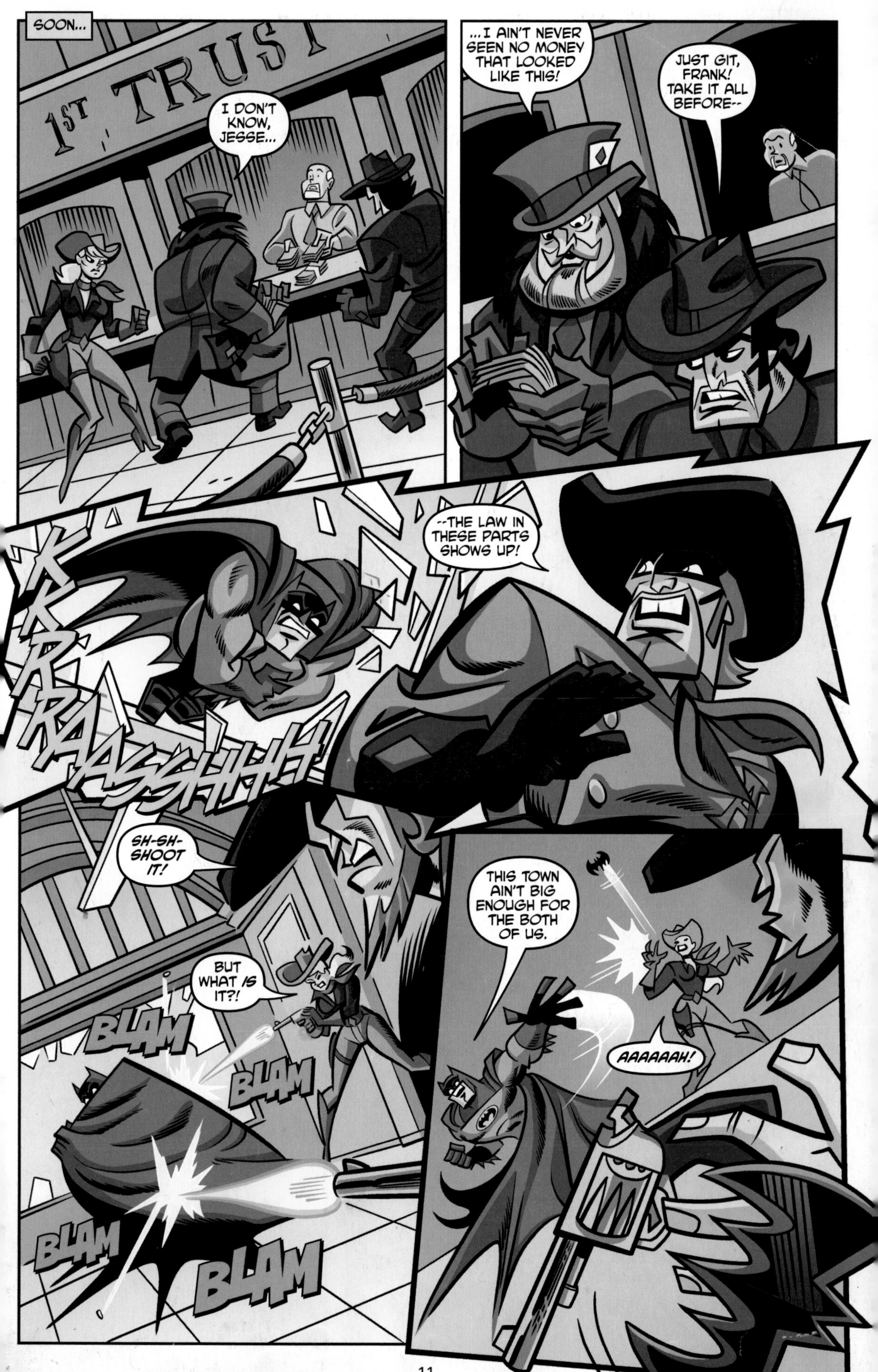
SOON...
1ST TRUST
I DON'T KNOW, JESSE...
...I AIN'T NEVER SEEN NO MONEY THAT LOOKED LIKE THIS!
JUST GIT, FRANK! TAKE IT ALL BEFORE--
--THE LAW IN THESE PARTS SHOWS UP!
KKRRAASSHHHH
SH-SH-SHOOT IT!
BUT WHAT IS IT?!
BLAM
BLAM
BLAM
BLAM
THIS TOWN AIN'T BIG ENOUGH FOR THE BOTH OF US.
AAAAAAH!

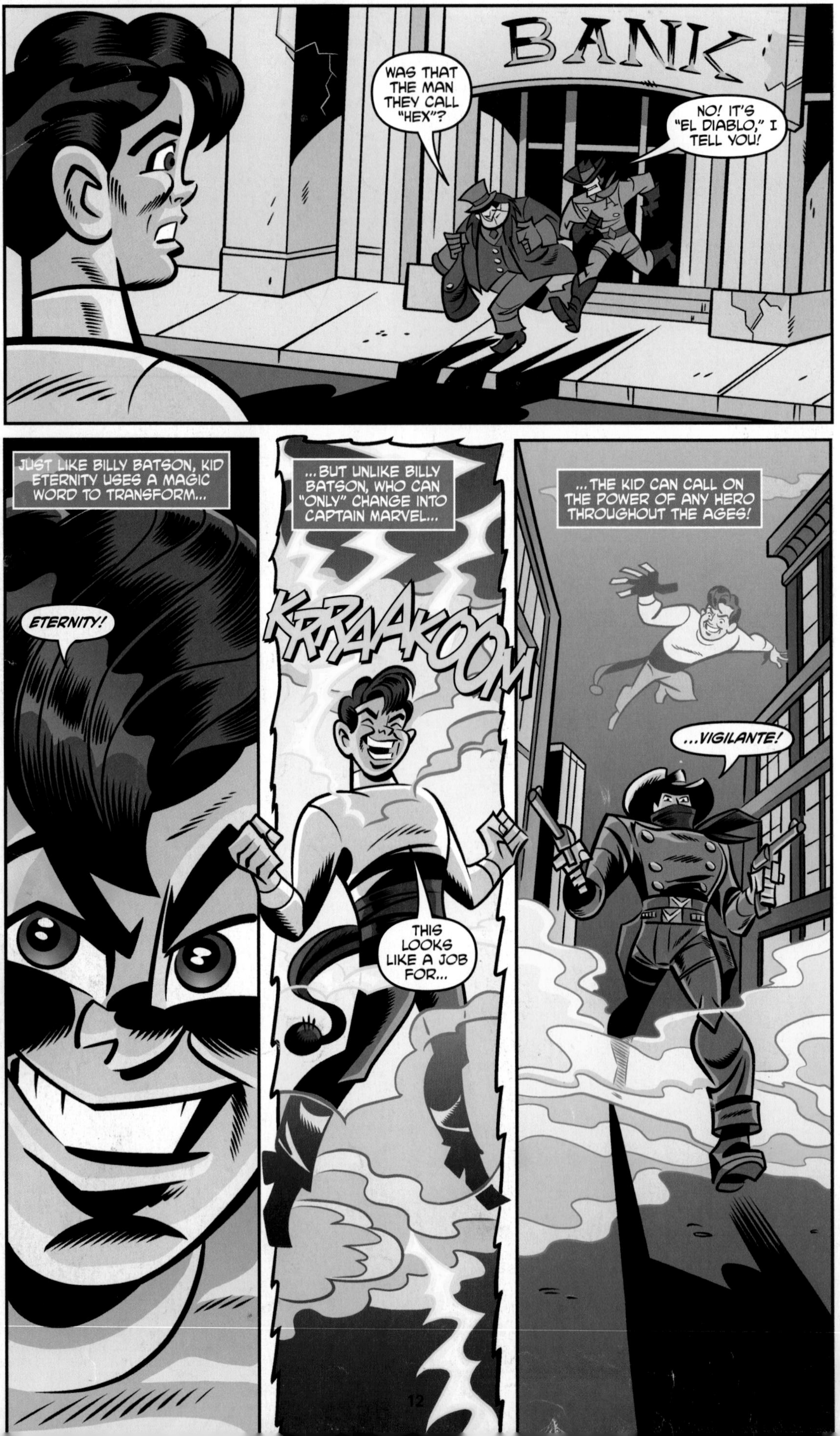
BANK
WAS THAT THE MAN THEY CALL "HEX"?
NO! IT'S "EL DIABLO," I TELL YOU!
JUST LIKE BILLY BATSON, KID ETERNITY USES A MAGIC WORD TO TRANSFORM...
ETERNITY!
...BUT UNLIKE BILLY BATSON, WHO CAN "ONLY" CHANGE INTO CAPTAIN MARVEL...
KRRAAKOOM
THIS LOOKS LIKE A JOB FOR...
...THE KID CAN CALL ON THE POWER OF ANY HERO THROUGHOUT THE AGES!
...VIGILANTE!

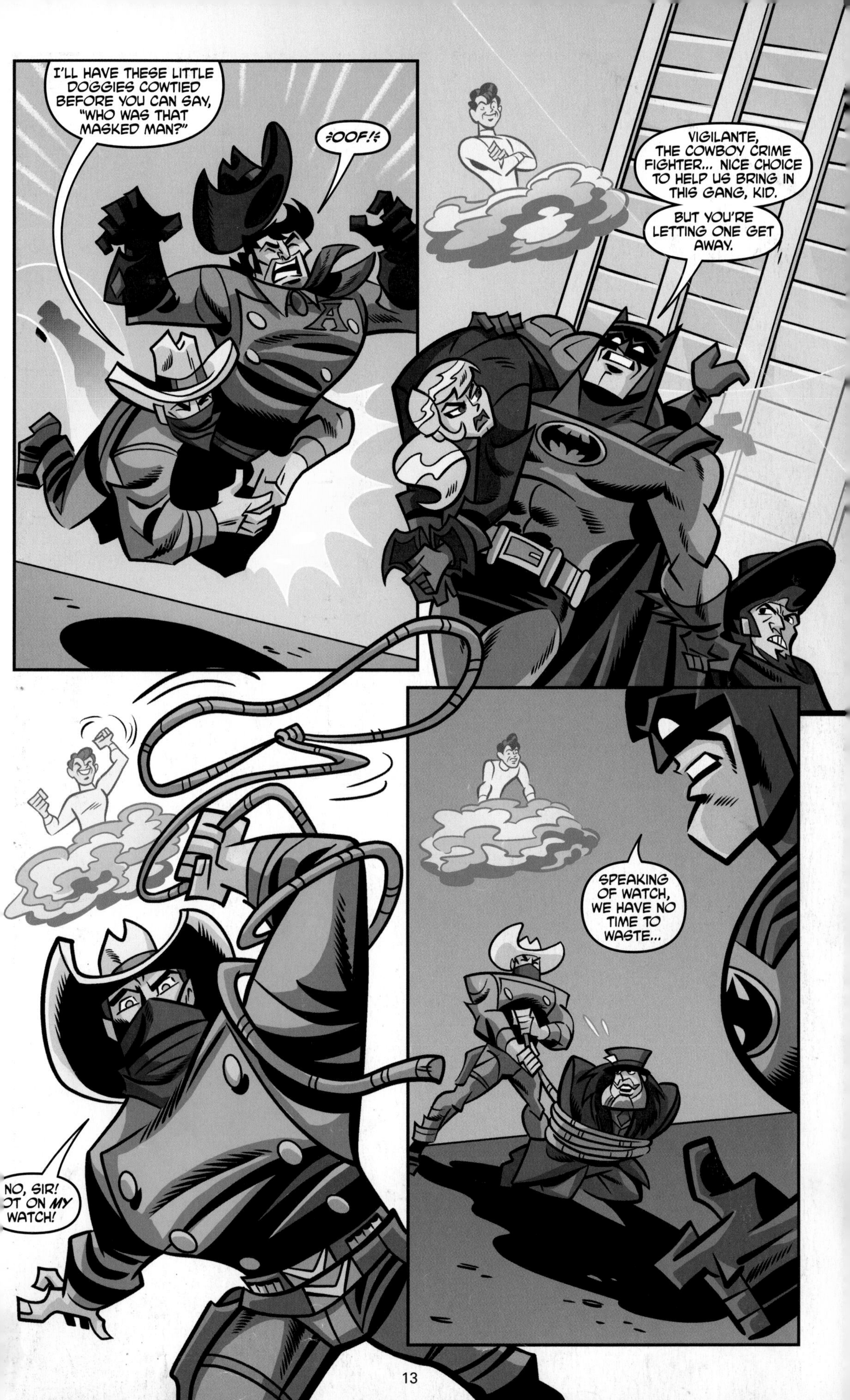
I'LL HAVE THESE LITTLE DOGGIES COWTIED BEFORE YOU CAN SAY, "WHO WAS THAT MASKED MAN?"
OOF!
VIGILANTE, THE COWBOY CRIME FIGHTER... NICE CHOICE TO HELP US BRING IN THIS GANG, KID.
BUT YOU'RE LETTING ONE GET AWAY.
NO, SIR!
OT ON MY WATCH!
SPEAKING OF WATCH, WE HAVE NO TIME TO WASTE...

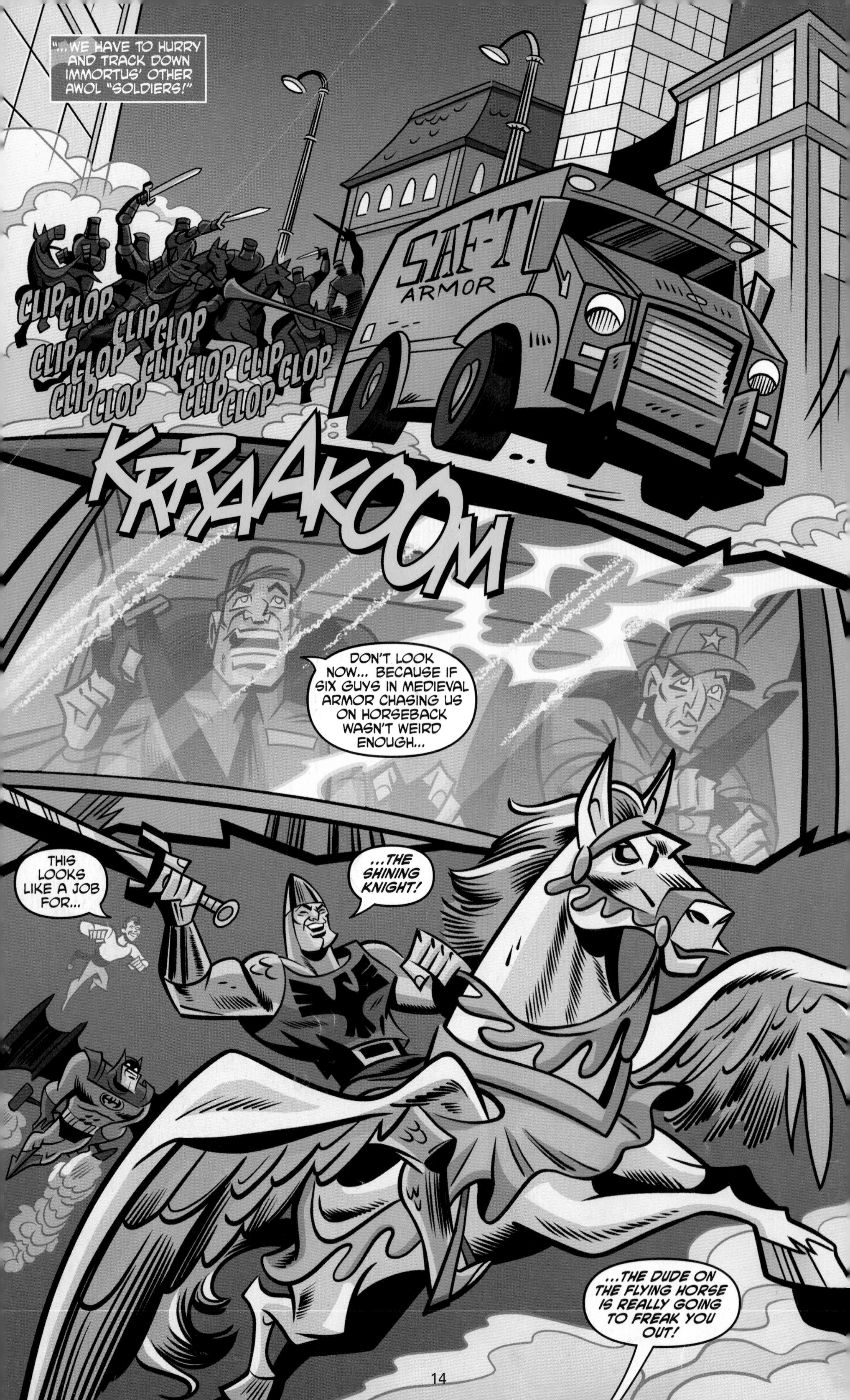

"...WE HAVE TO HURRY AND TRACK DOWN IMMORTUS' OTHER AWOL "SOLDIERS!"
SAF-T ARMOR
CLIP CLOP CLIP CLOP CLIP CLOP CLIP CLOP CLIP CLOP CLIP CLOP CLIP CLOP CLIP CLOP
KRRAAKOOM
DON'T LOOK NOW... BECAUSE IF SIX GUYS IN MEDIEVAL ARMOR CHASING US ON HORSEBACK WASN'T WEIRD ENOUGH...
THIS LOOKS LIKE A JOB FOR...
...THE SHINING KNIGHT!
...THE DUDE ON THE FLYING HORSE IS REALLY GOING TO FREAK YOU OUT!

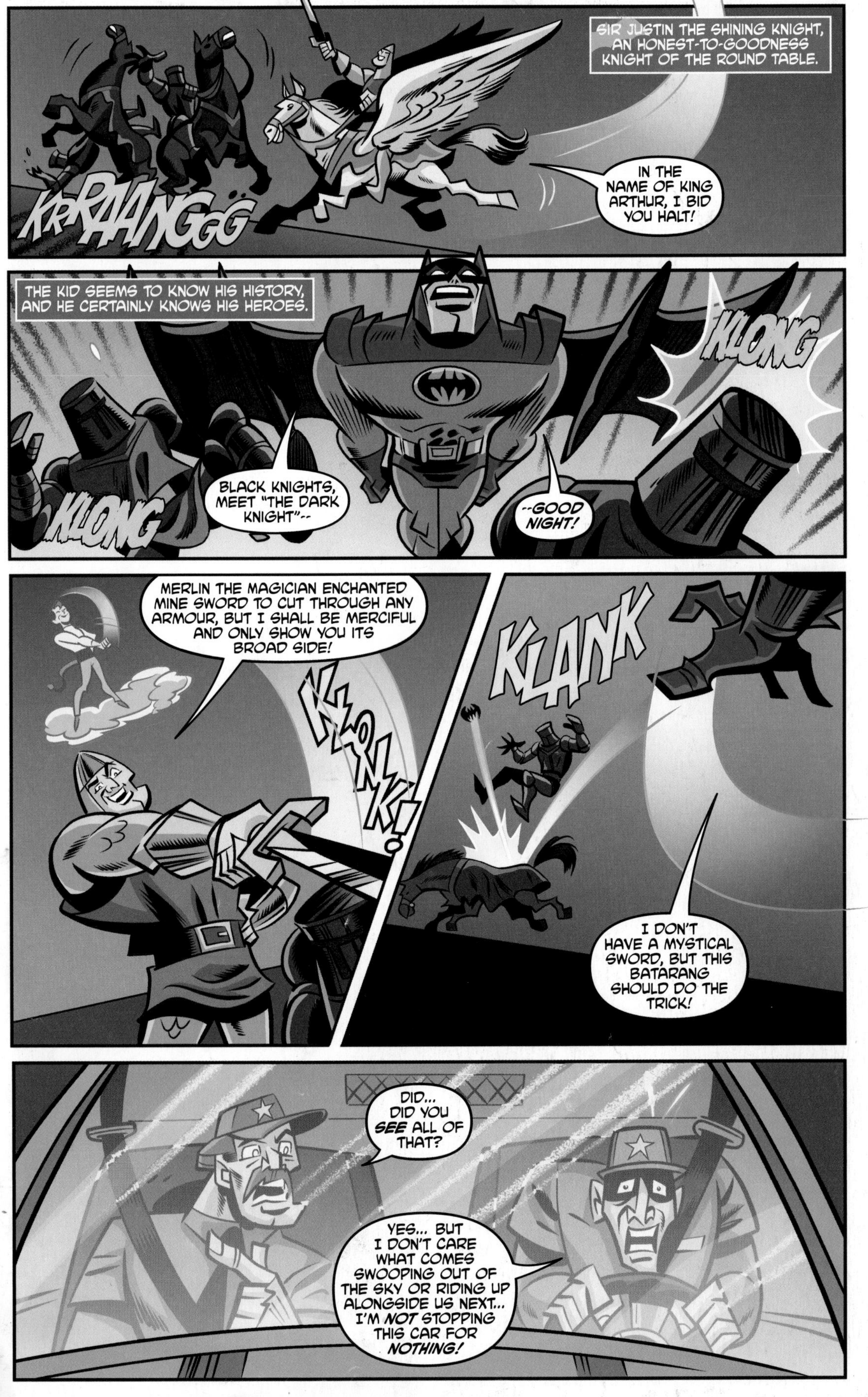
SIR JUSTIN THE SHINING KNIGHT, AN HONEST-TO-GOODNESS KNIGHT OF THE ROUND TABLE.
KRRAANGGG
IN THE NAME OF KING ARTHUR, I BID YOU HALT!
THE KID SEEMS TO KNOW HIS HISTORY, AND HE CERTAINLY KNOWS HIS HEROES.
KLONG
BLACK KNIGHTS, MEET "THE DARK KNIGHT"--
KLONG
--GOOD NIGHT!
MERLIN THE MAGICIAN ENCHANTED MINE SWORD TO CUT THROUGH ANY ARMOUR, BUT I SHALL BE MERCIFUL AND ONLY SHOW YOU ITS BROAD SIDE!
KLONK!
KLANK
I DON'T HAVE A MYSTICAL SWORD, BUT THIS BATARANG SHOULD DO THE TRICK!
DID... DID YOU *SEE* ALL OF THAT?
YES... BUT I DON'T CARE WHAT COMES SWOOPING OUT OF THE SKY OR RIDING UP ALONGSIDE US NEXT... I'M *NOT* STOPPING THIS CAR FOR *NOTHING!*

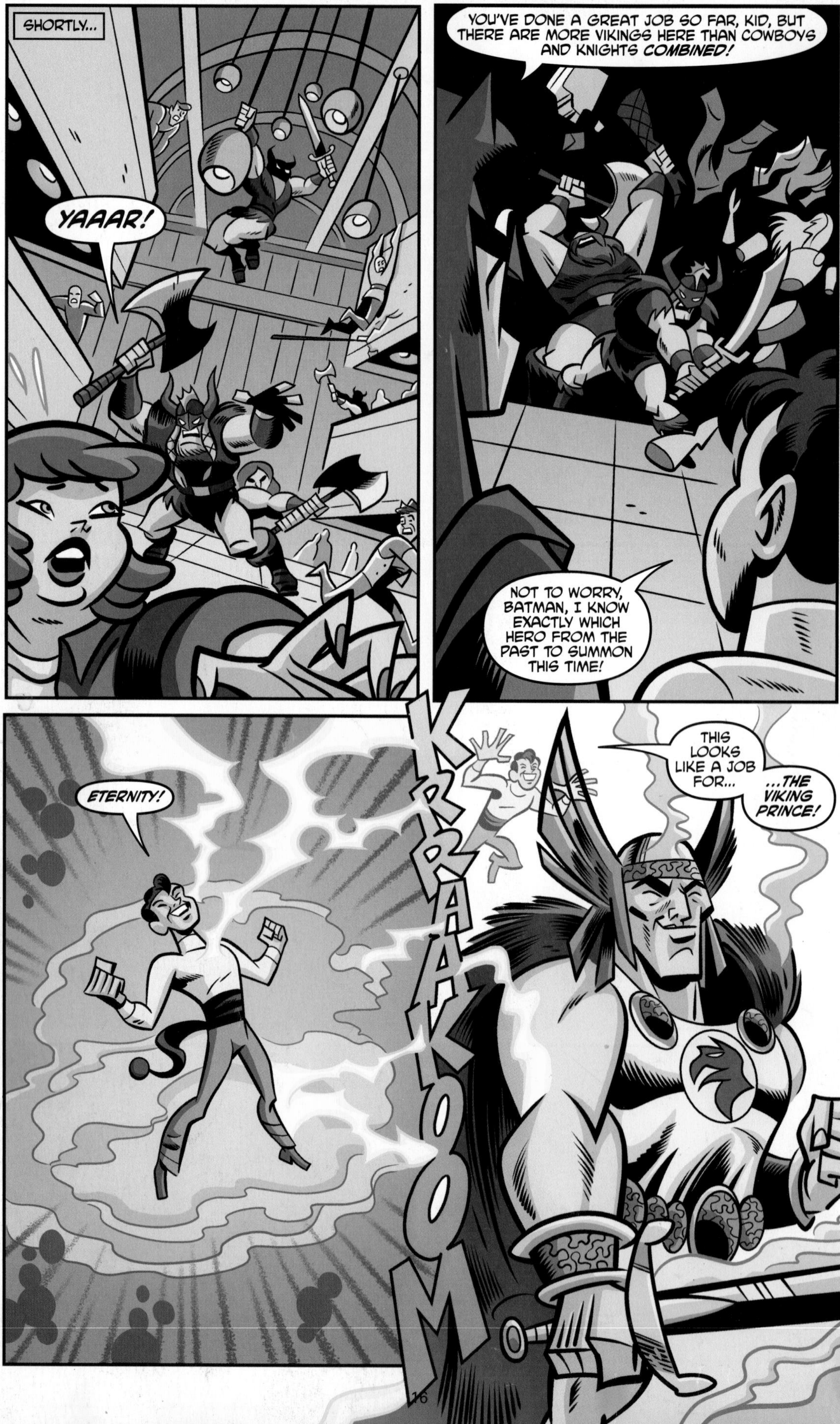
SHORTLY...
YAAAR!
YOU'VE DONE A GREAT JOB SO FAR, KID, BUT THERE ARE MORE VIKINGS HERE THAN COWBOYS AND KNIGHTS COMBINED!
NOT TO WORRY, BATMAN, I KNOW EXACTLY WHICH HERO FROM THE PAST TO SUMMON THIS TIME!
ETERNITY!
KRRAAAKOOOM
THIS LOOKS LIKE A JOB FOR...
...THE VIKING PRINCE!

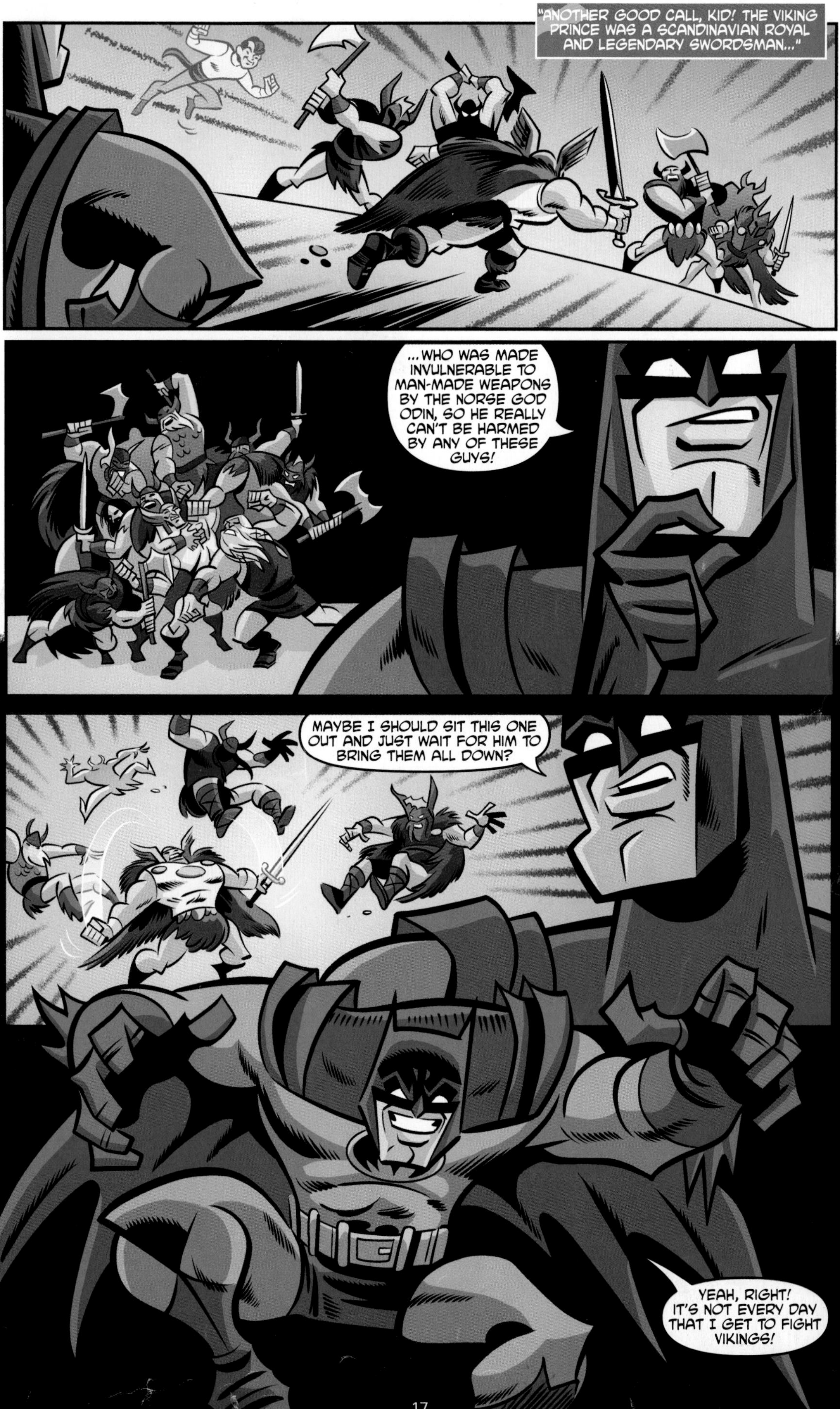
"ANOTHER GOOD CALL, KID! THE VIKING PRINCE WAS A SCANDINAVIAN ROYAL AND LEGENDARY SWORDSMAN..."
...WHO WAS MADE INVULNERABLE TO MAN-MADE WEAPONS BY THE NORSE GOD ODIN, SO HE REALLY CAN'T BE HARMED BY ANY OF THESE GUYS!
MAYBE I SHOULD SIT THIS ONE OUT AND JUST WAIT FOR HIM TO BRING THEM ALL DOWN?
YEAH, RIGHT! IT'S NOT EVERY DAY THAT I GET TO FIGHT VIKINGS!

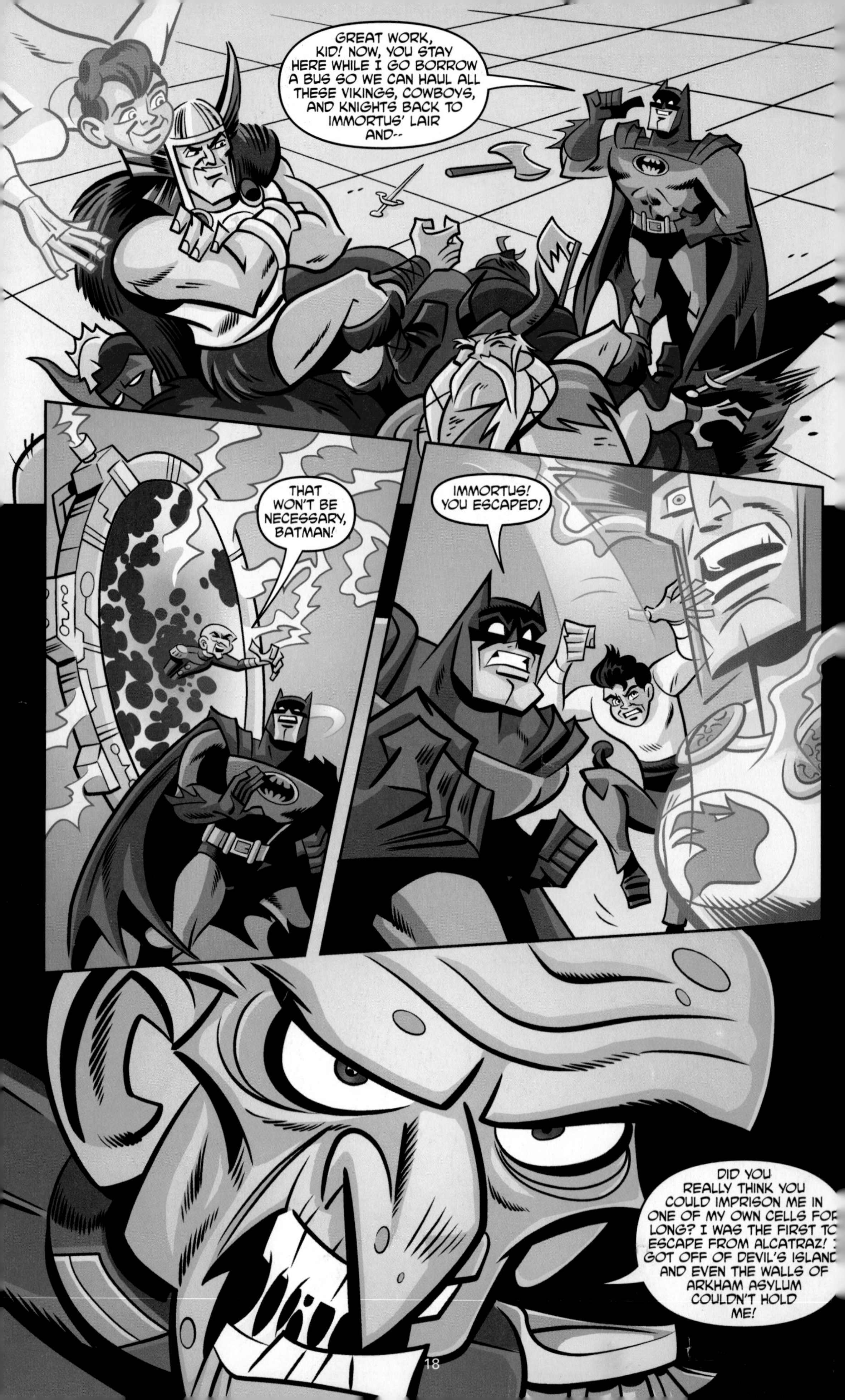
GREAT WORK, KID! NOW, YOU STAY HERE WHILE I GO BORROW A BUS SO WE CAN HAUL ALL THESE VIKINGS, COWBOYS, AND KNIGHTS BACK TO IMMORTUS' LAIR AND--
THAT WON'T BE NECESSARY, BATMAN!
IMMORTUS! YOU ESCAPED!
DID YOU REALLY THINK YOU COULD IMPRISON ME IN ONE OF MY OWN CELLS FOR LONG? I WAS THE FIRST TO ESCAPE FROM ALCATRAZ! I GOT OFF OF DEVIL'S ISLAND AND EVEN THE WALLS OF ARKHAM ASYLUM COULDN'T HOLD ME!

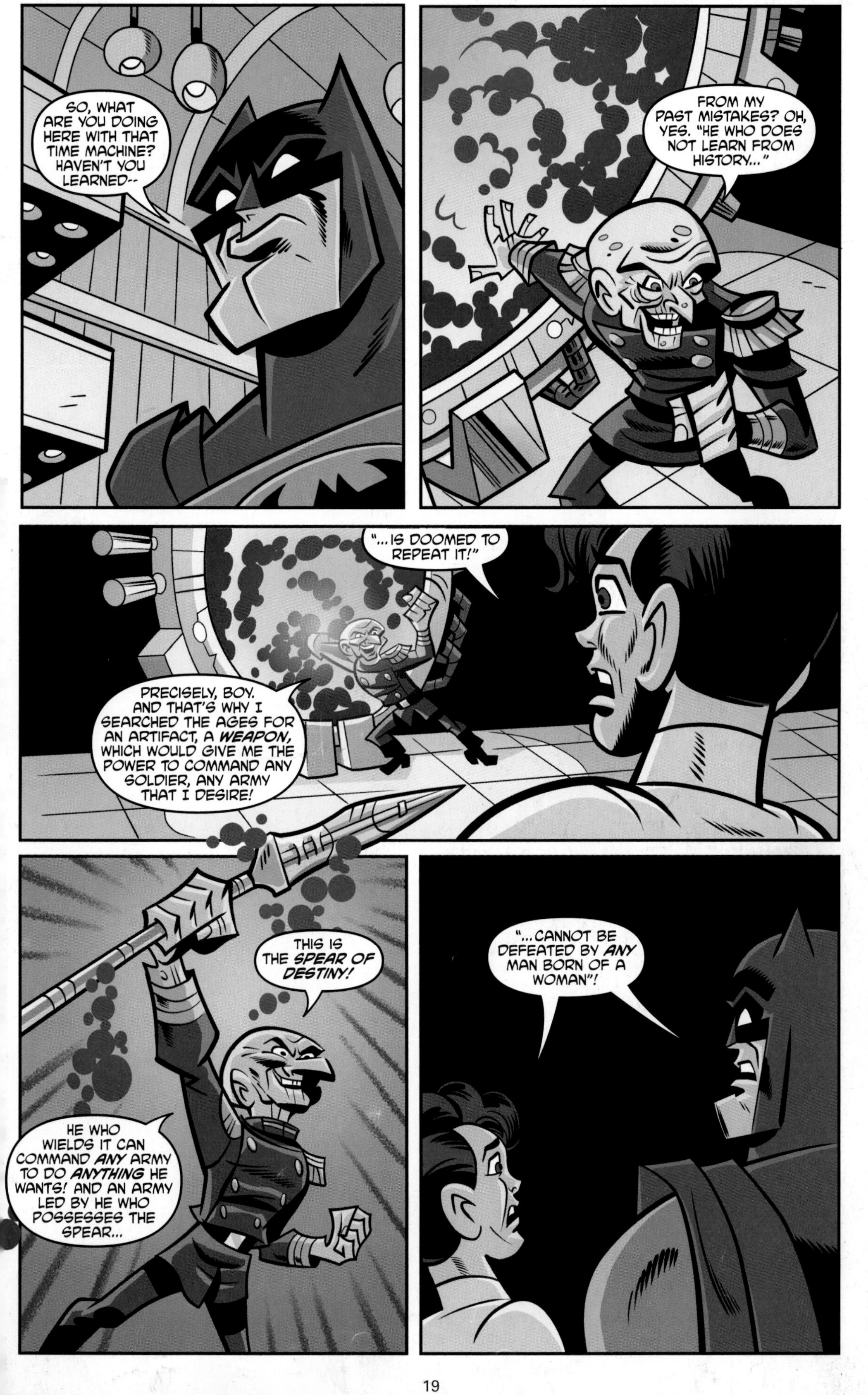
SO, WHAT ARE YOU DOING HERE WITH THAT TIME MACHINE? HAVEN'T YOU LEARNED--
FROM MY PAST MISTAKES? OH, YES. "HE WHO DOES NOT LEARN FROM HISTORY..."
"...IS DOOMED TO REPEAT IT!"
PRECISELY, BOY. AND THAT'S WHY I SEARCHED THE AGES FOR AN ARTIFACT, A WEAPON, WHICH WOULD GIVE ME THE POWER TO COMMAND ANY SOLDIER, ANY ARMY THAT I DESIRE!
THIS IS THE SPEAR OF DESTINY!
HE WHO WIELDS IT CAN COMMAND ANY ARMY TO DO ANYTHING HE WANTS! AND AN ARMY LED BY HE WHO POSSESSES THE SPEAR...
"...CANNOT BE DEFEATED BY ANY MAN BORN OF A WOMAN"!

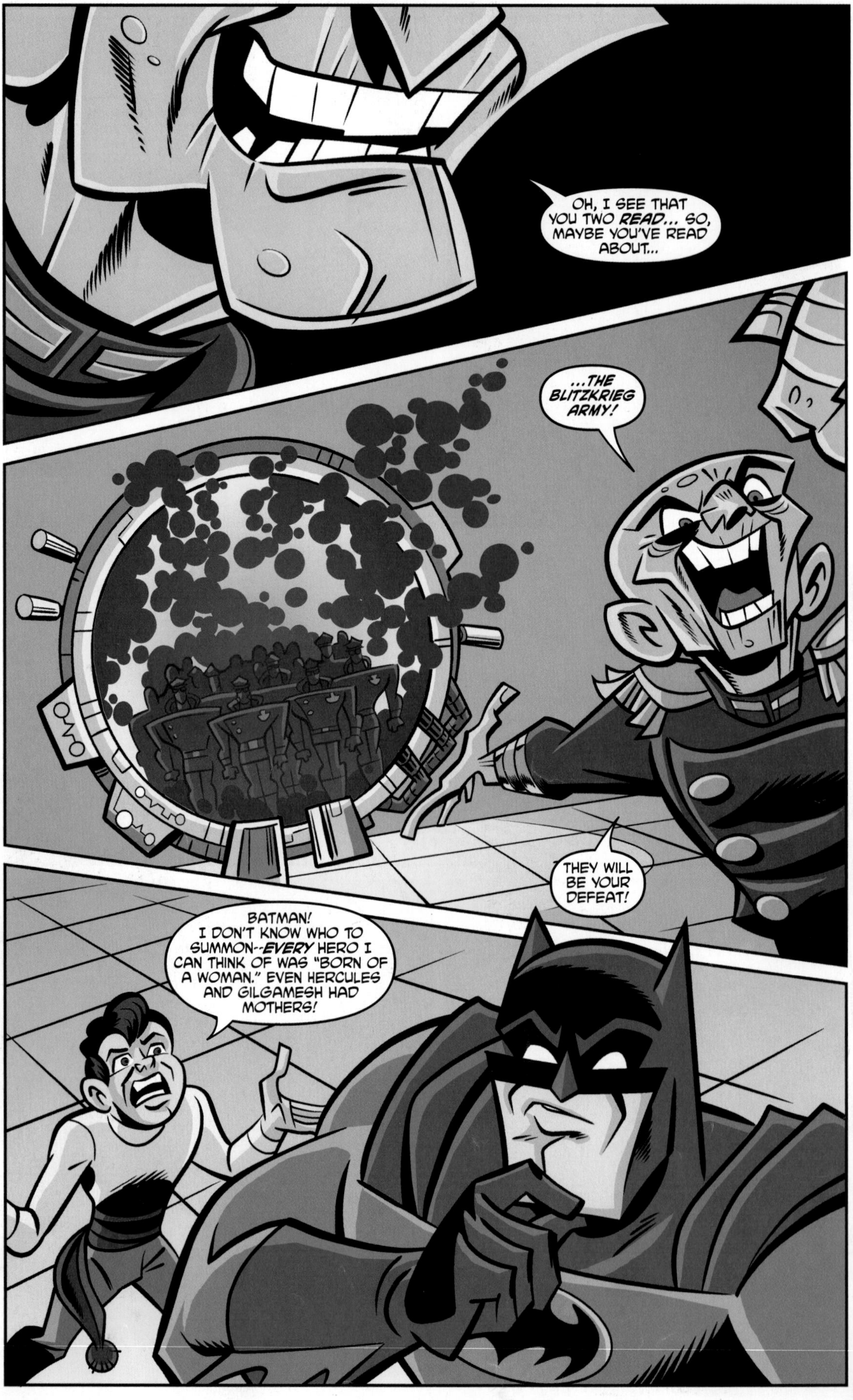
OH, I SEE THAT YOU TWO *READ*... SO, MAYBE YOU'VE READ ABOUT...
...*THE BLITZKRIEG ARMY!*
THEY WILL BE YOUR DEFEAT!
BATMAN! I DON'T KNOW WHO TO SUMMON--*EVERY* HERO I CAN THINK OF WAS "BORN OF A WOMAN." EVEN HERCULES AND GILGAMESH HAD MOTHERS!

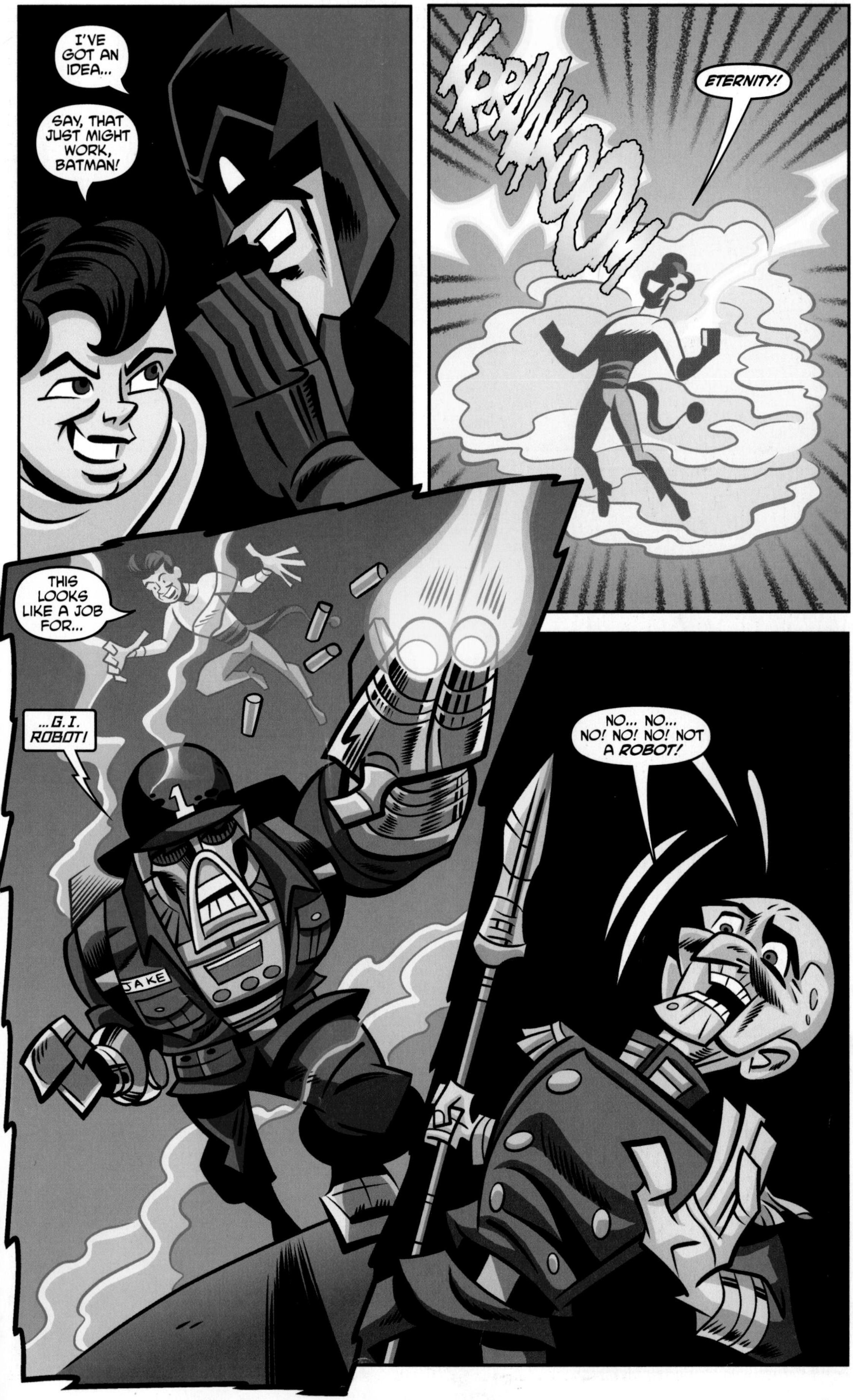
I'VE GOT AN IDEA...
SAY, THAT JUST MIGHT WORK, BATMAN!
KRAKOOM
ETERNITY!
THIS LOOKS LIKE A JOB FOR...
...G.I. ROBOT!
NO... NO... NO! NO! NO! NOT A ROBOT!
JAKE

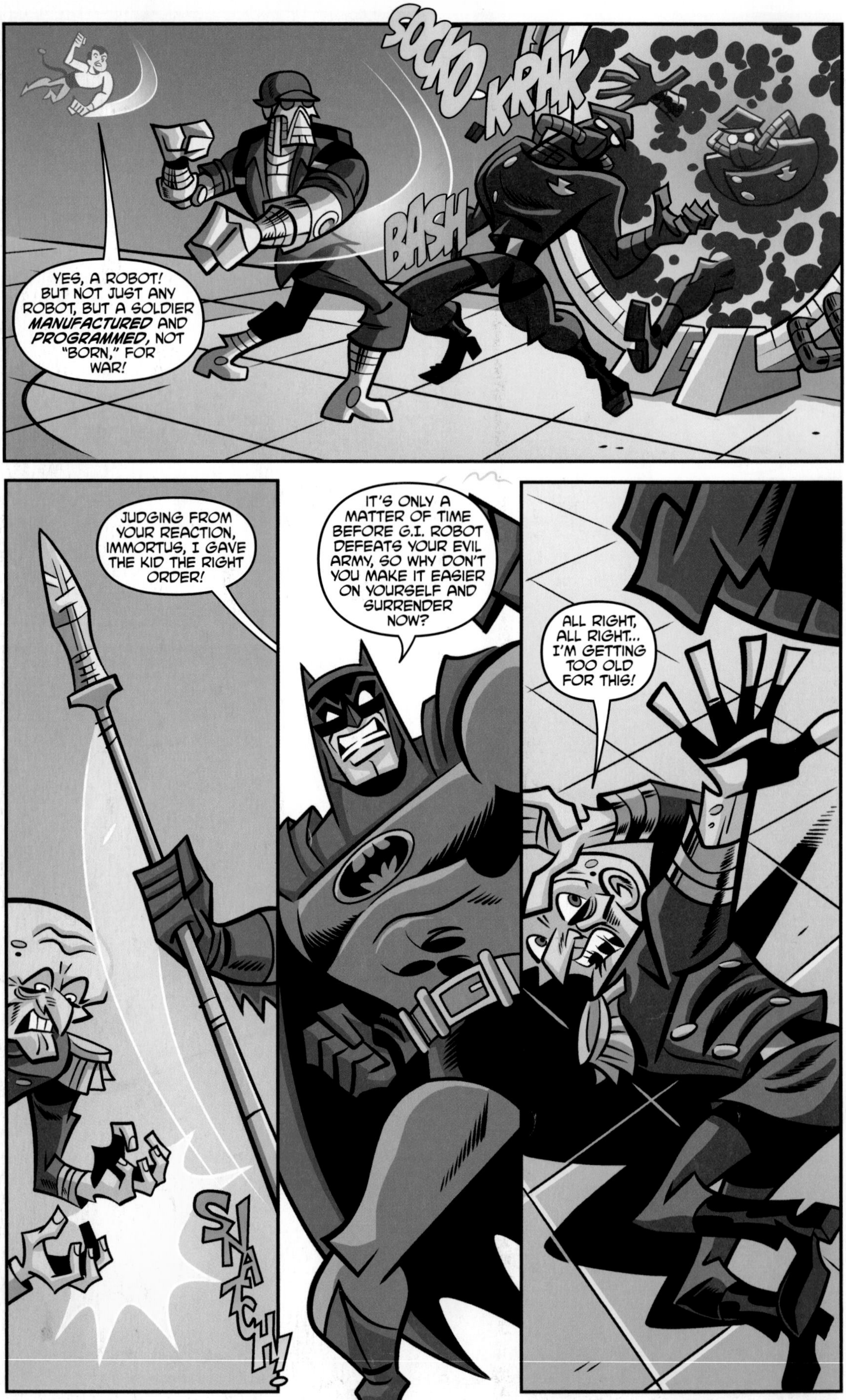
SOCKO
KRAK
BASH
YES, A ROBOT! BUT NOT JUST ANY ROBOT, BUT A SOLDIER *MANUFACTURED* AND *PROGRAMMED*, NOT "BORN," FOR WAR!
JUDGING FROM YOUR REACTION, IMMORTUS, I GAVE THE KID THE RIGHT ORDER!
SNATCH!
IT'S ONLY A MATTER OF TIME BEFORE G.I. ROBOT DEFEATS YOUR EVIL ARMY, SO WHY DON'T YOU MAKE IT EASIER ON YOURSELF AND SURRENDER NOW?
ALL RIGHT, ALL RIGHT... I'M GETTING TOO OLD FOR THIS!

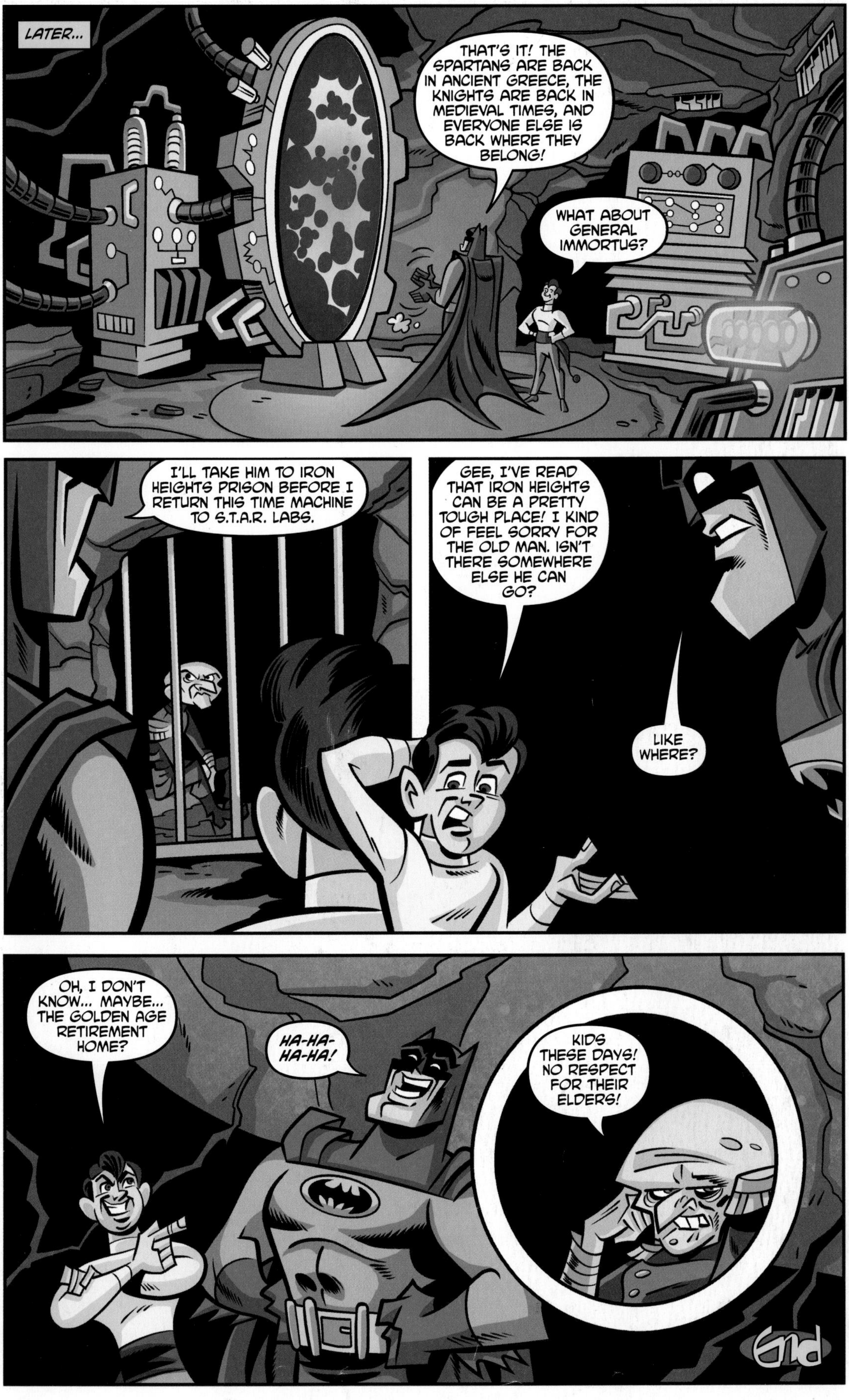
LATER...
THAT'S IT! THE SPARTANS ARE BACK IN ANCIENT GREECE, THE KNIGHTS ARE BACK IN MEDIEVAL TIMES, AND EVERYONE ELSE IS BACK WHERE THEY BELONG!
WHAT ABOUT GENERAL IMMORTUS?
I'LL TAKE HIM TO IRON HEIGHTS PRISON BEFORE I RETURN THIS TIME MACHINE TO S.T.A.R. LABS.
GEE, I'VE READ THAT IRON HEIGHTS CAN BE A PRETTY TOUGH PLACE! I KIND OF FEEL SORRY FOR THE OLD MAN. ISN'T THERE SOMEWHERE ELSE HE CAN GO?
LIKE WHERE?
OH, I DON'T KNOW... MAYBE... THE GOLDEN AGE RETIREMENT HOME?
HA-HA-HA-HA!
KIDS THESE DAYS! NO RESPECT FOR THEIR ELDERS!
End

GENERAL IMMORTUS

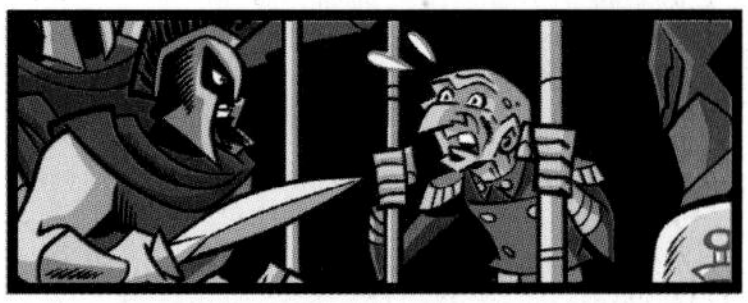

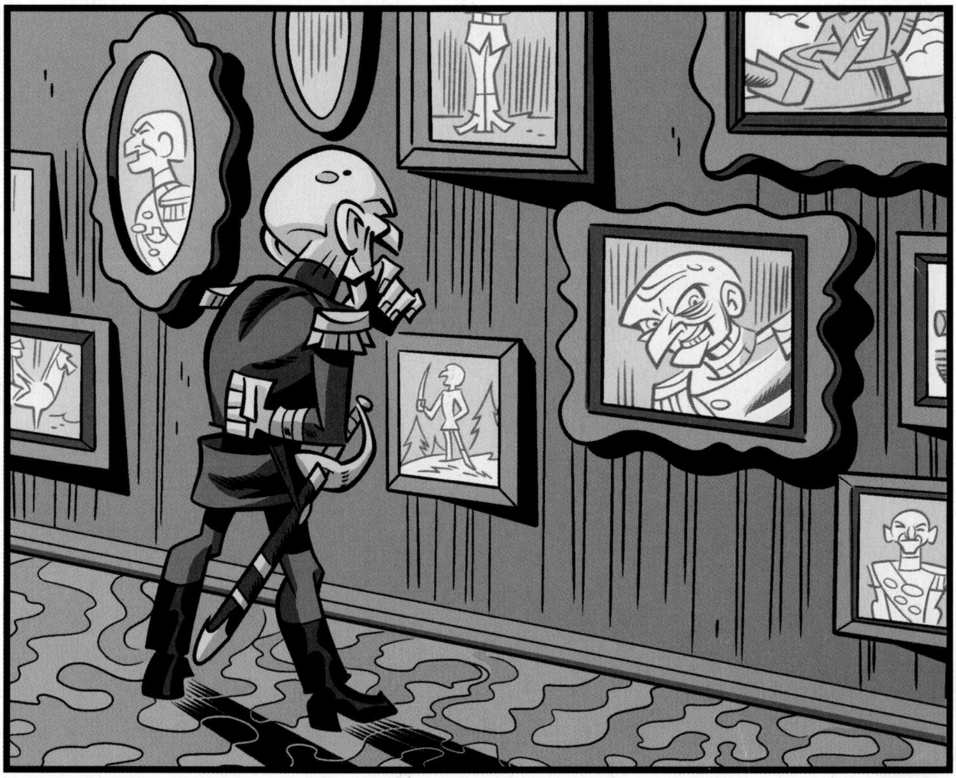

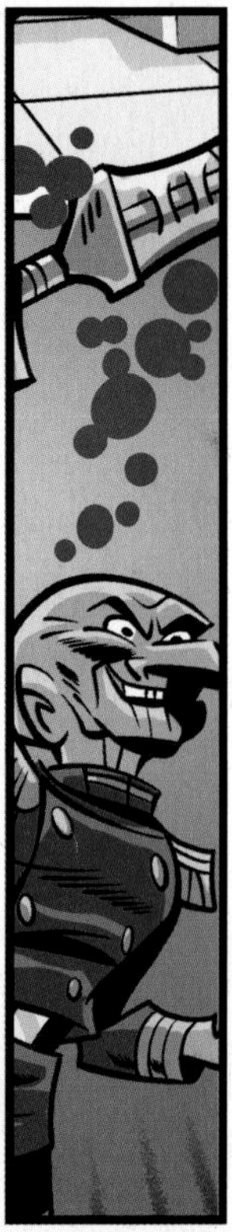

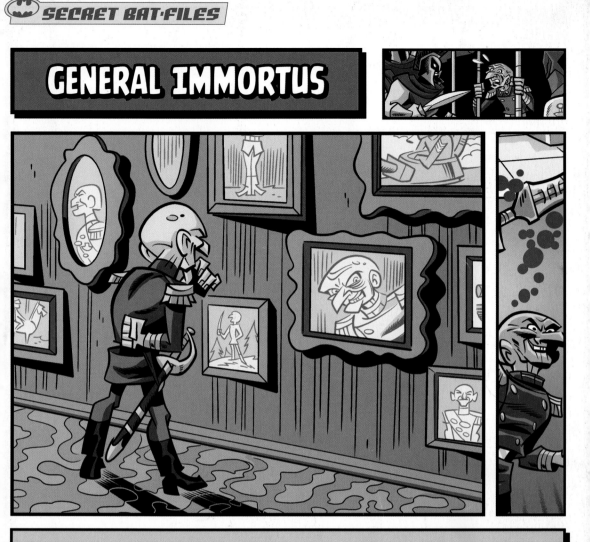

General Immortus has lived for centuries due to a secret "life-extending potion." He has spent his very long life fighting on the wrong side of various wars, including the war on crime.

TOP SECRET:
Also known as the "Forever Soldier," General Immortus seems forever doomed to repeat the mistakes of his past crimes, time and time again.

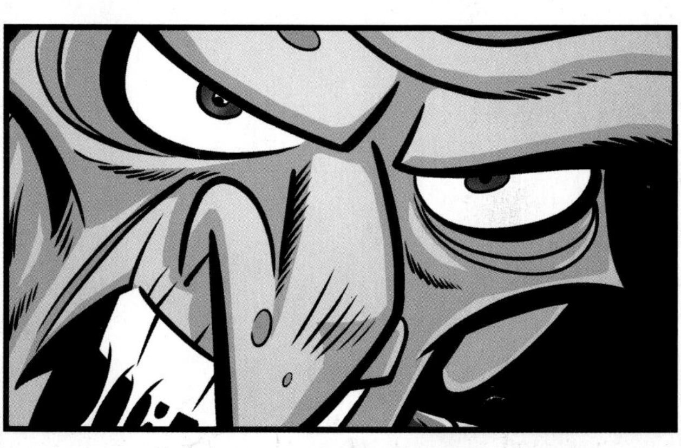

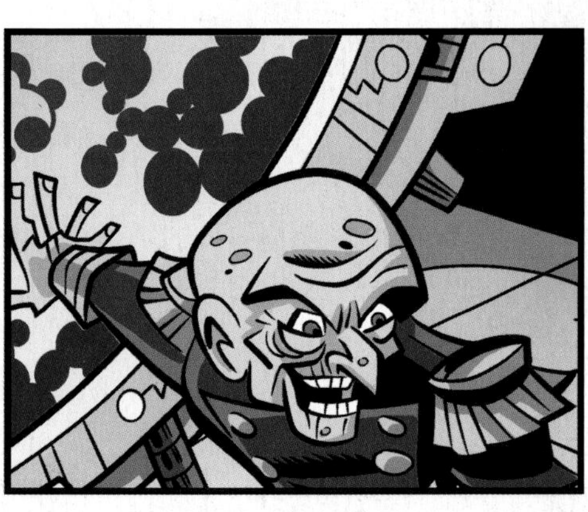

KID ETERNITY

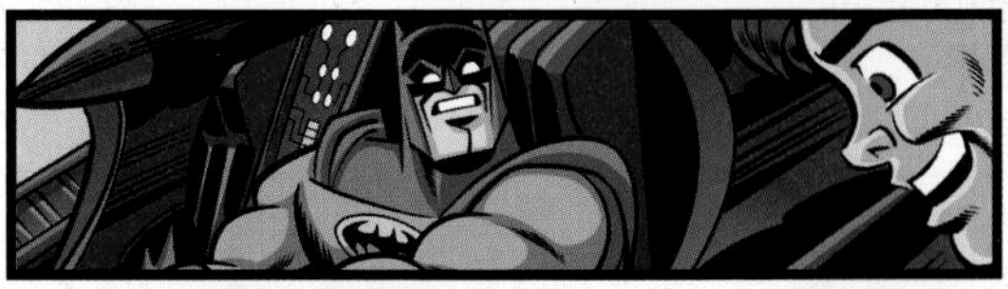

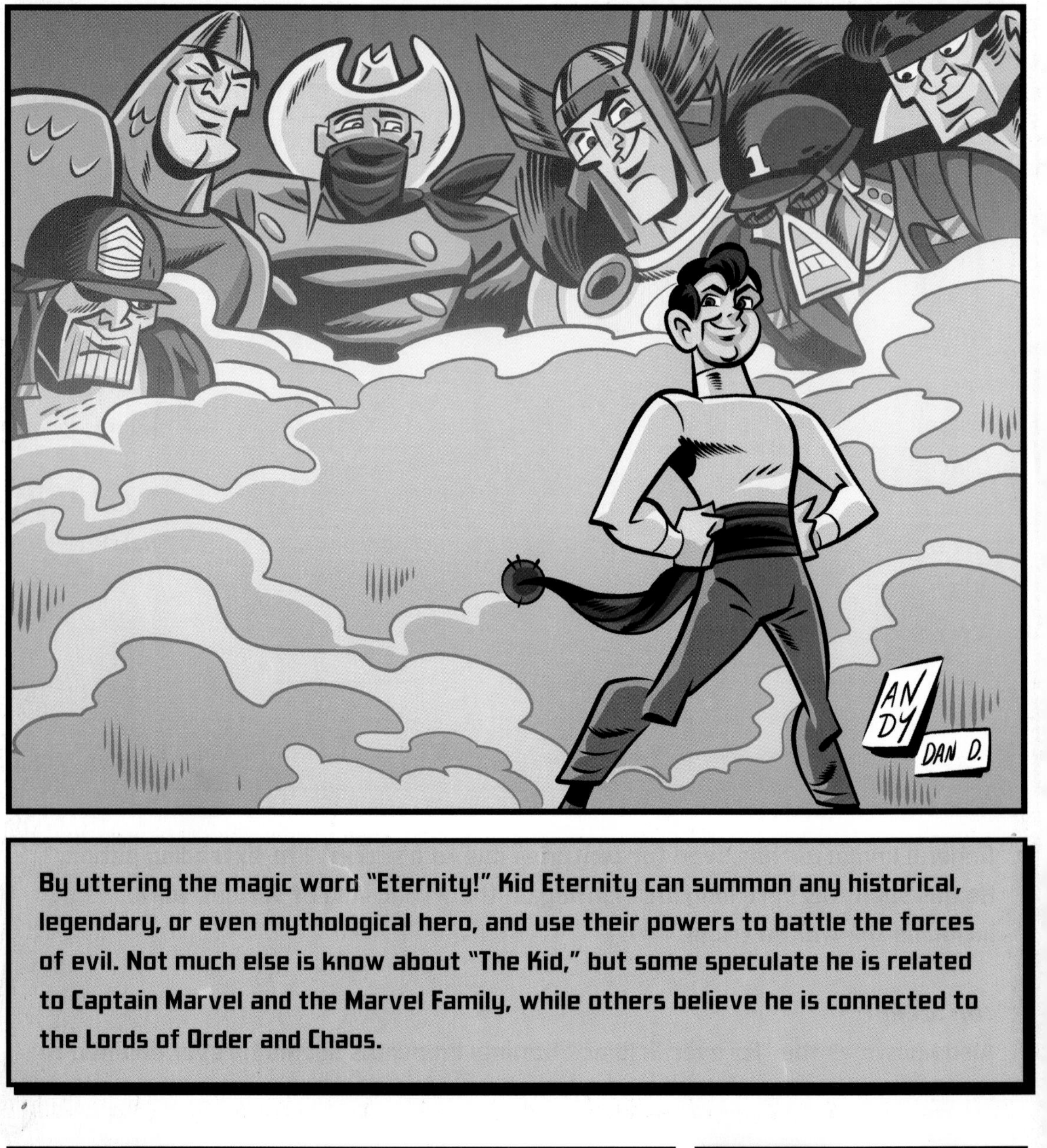
ANDY
DAN D.

By uttering the magic word "Eternity!" Kid Eternity can summon any historical, legendary, or even mythological hero, and use their powers to battle the forces of evil. Not much else is know about "The Kid," but some speculate he is related to Captain Marvel and the Marvel Family, while others believe he is connected to the Lords of Order and Chaos.

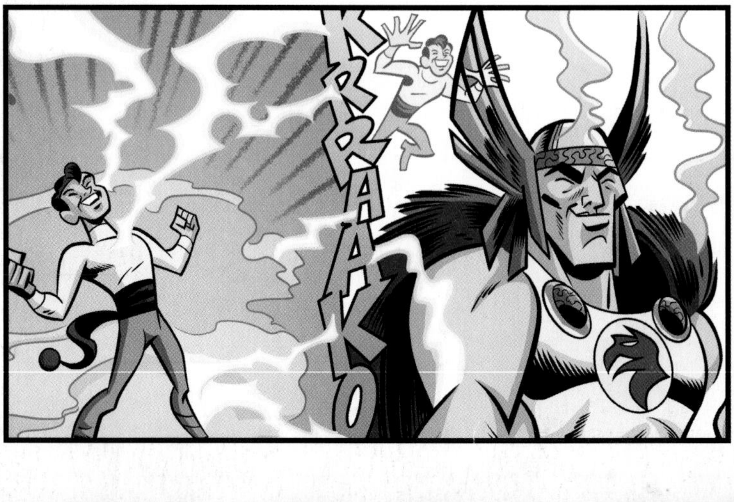
KRRAAKO

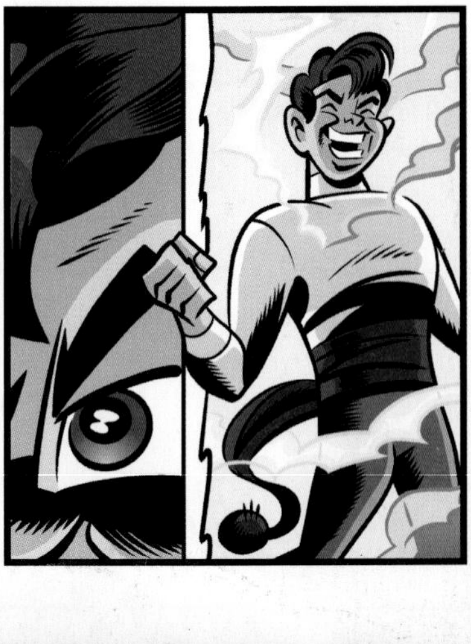

CREATORS

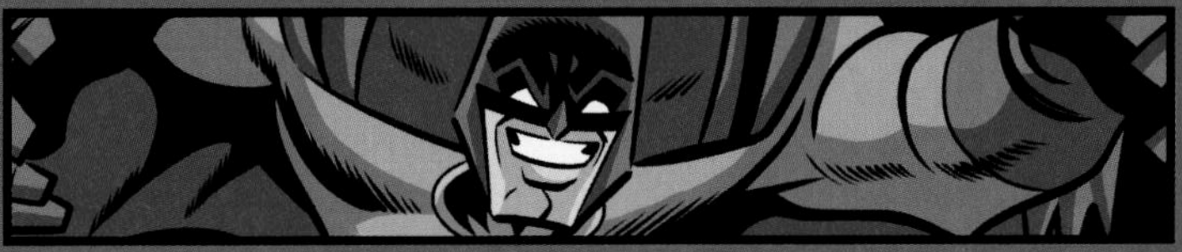

J. TORRES WRITER

J. Torres won the Shuster Award for Outstanding Writer for his work on *Batman: Legends of the Dark Knight*, *Love As a Foreign Language*, and *Teen Titans Go*. He is also the writer of the Eisner Award nominated *Alison Dare* and the YALSA listed *Days Like This* and *Lola: A Ghost Story*. Other comic book credits include *Avatar: The Last Airbender*, *Legion of Super-Heroes in the 31st Century*, *Ninja Scroll*, *Wonder Girl*, *Wonder Woman*, and *WALL-E: Recharge.*

ANDY SURIANO PENCILLER

Andy Suriano is an illustrator of both comic books and animation. His comic book credits include *Batman: The Brave and the Bold* and *Doc Bizarre, M.D.* He's worked on popular animated television series as well, such as *Samurai Jack* and *Star Wars: The Clone Wars.*

DAN DAVIS INKER

Dan Davis is a comic illustrator for DC Comics, Warner Bros., and Bongo. His work has been nominated for several Eisner Awards, including his work on *Batman: The Brave and the Bold*. During his career, Davis has illustrated Batman, The Simpsons, Harry Potter, Samurai Jack, and many other well-known characters!

GLOSSARY

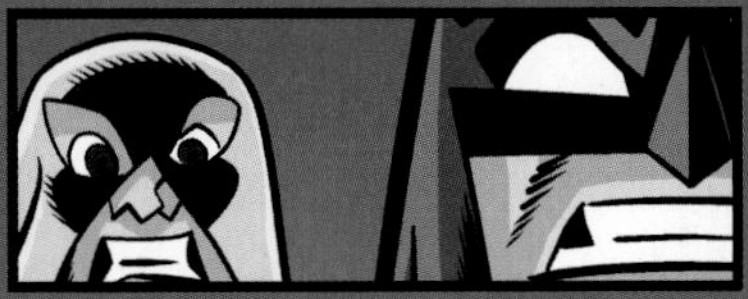

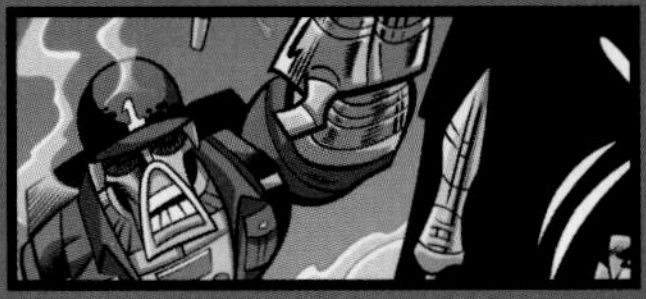

amok [uh-MUHK] - wild frenzy

artifact [ART-uh-fakt] - an object made in the past

distress [diss-TRESS] - a feeling of great pain or sadness

harebrained [HAIR-braynd] - foolish or absurd

insubordinate [in-suh-BORD-uhn-it] - not submitting to authority; rebellious

medieval [med-EE-vuhl] - to do with the Middle Ages, the period of history between A.D. 500 and 1450.

merciful [MUR-si-fuhl] - compassionate, lenient, or forgiving

spar [SPAHR] - strike or fight with another

VISUAL QUESTIONS & PROMPTS

1. Based on what you know about Kid Eternity from this comic book, what do you think he was studying at the library? Use specific panels to support your opinion.

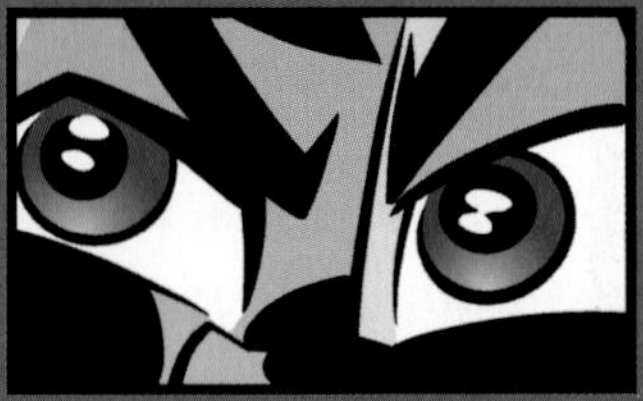

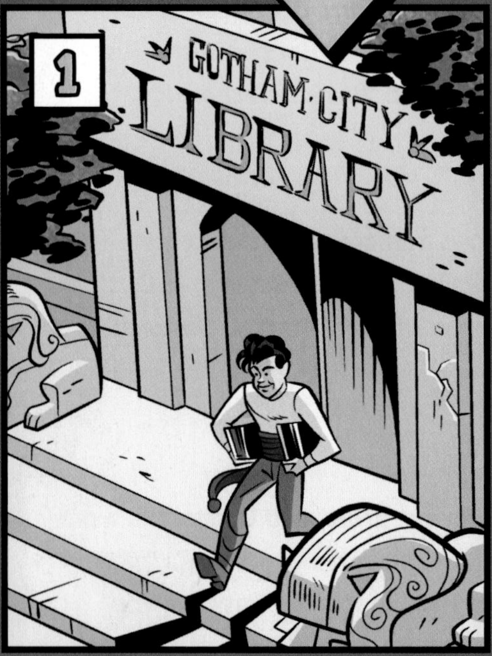
1
GOTHAM CITY
LIBRARY

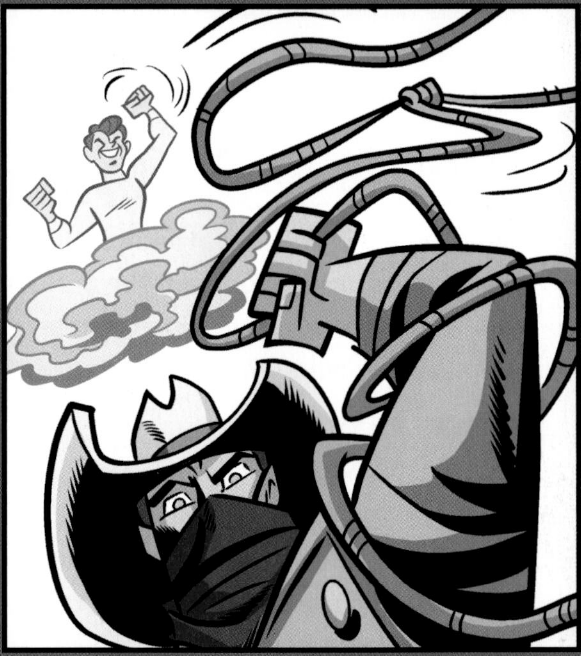

2. Based on what you know about General Immortus from this comic book, what probably happened in the panel at right? Why are the Spartans there? Why are they attacking the General?

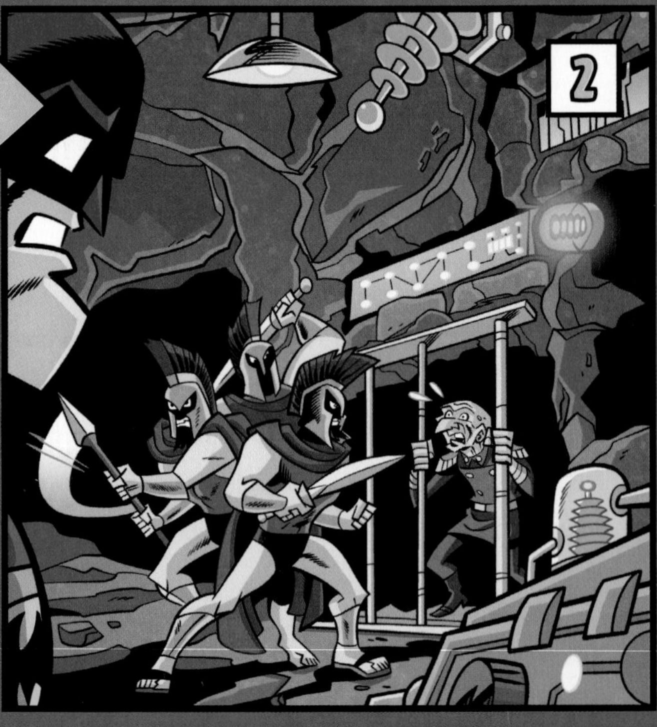
2

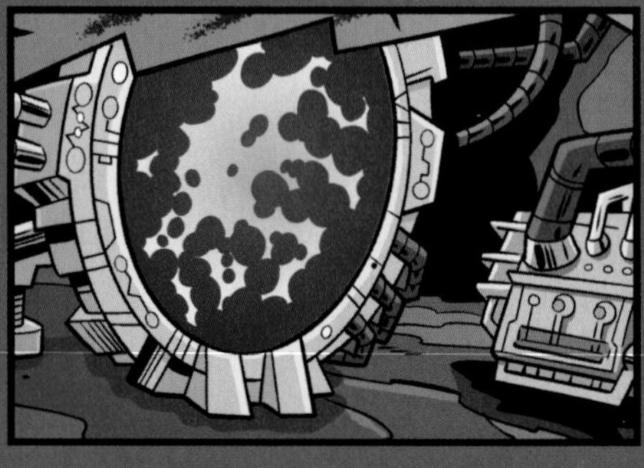

3. Why do you think Batman is colored solid black in this panel? How does Batman's appearance make you feel?

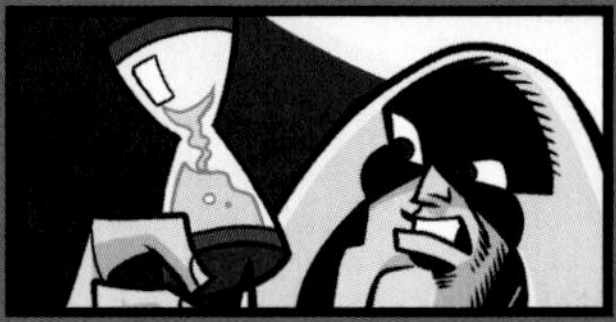

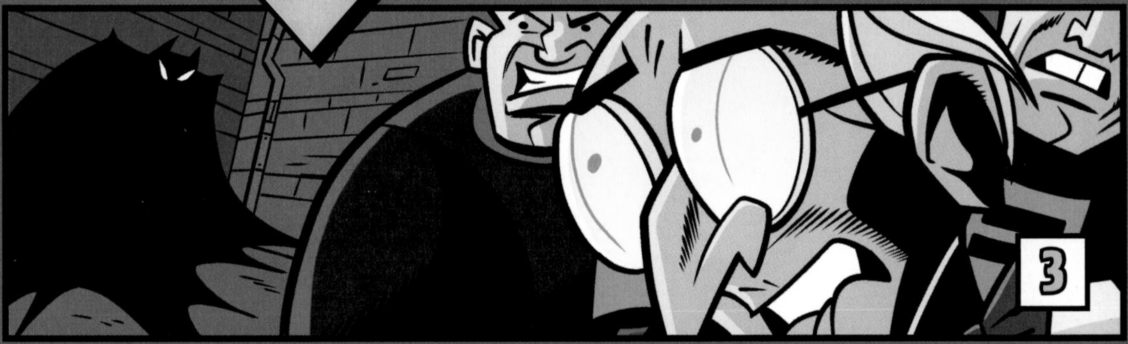
3

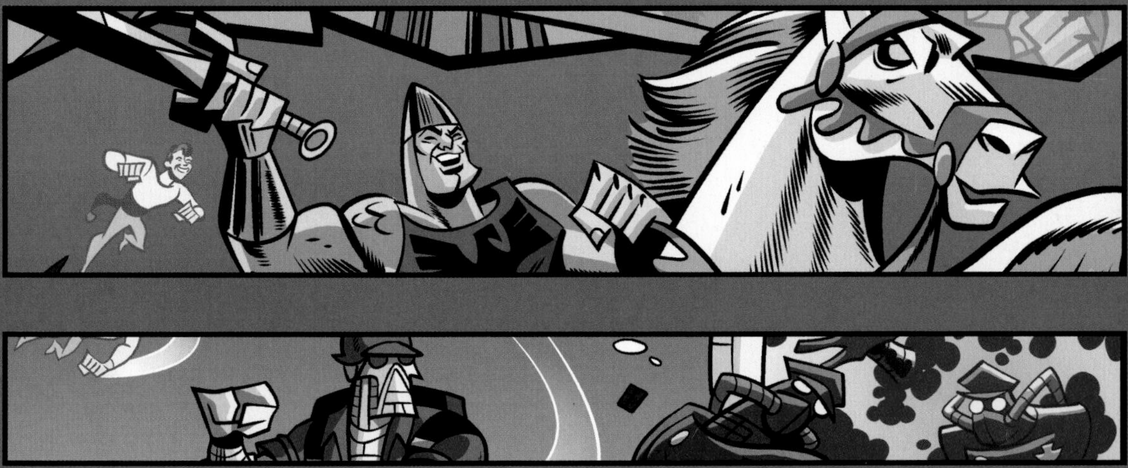

4. Why do you think the borders of this panel are jagged? What effect does it create?

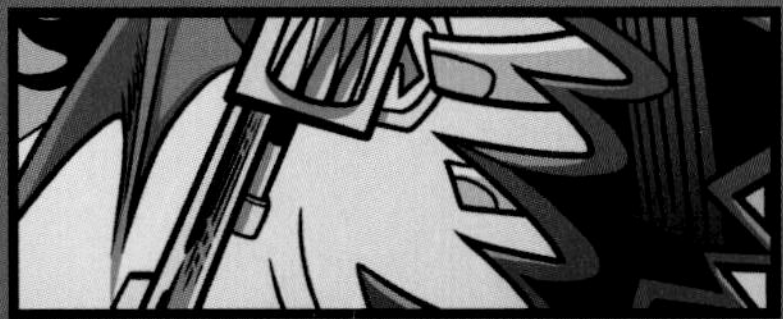

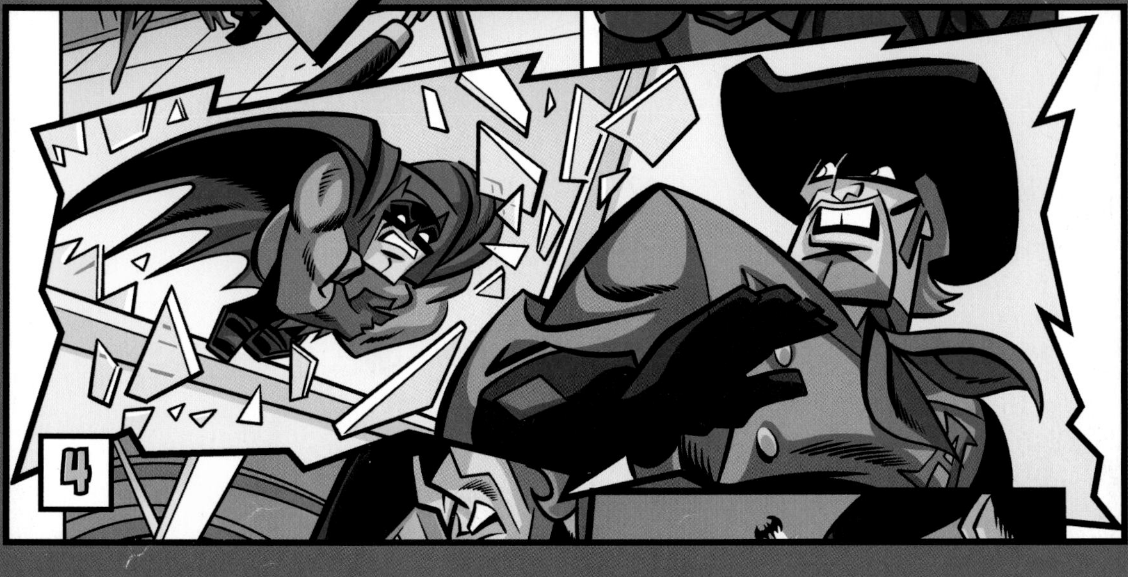
4

READ THEM ALL!

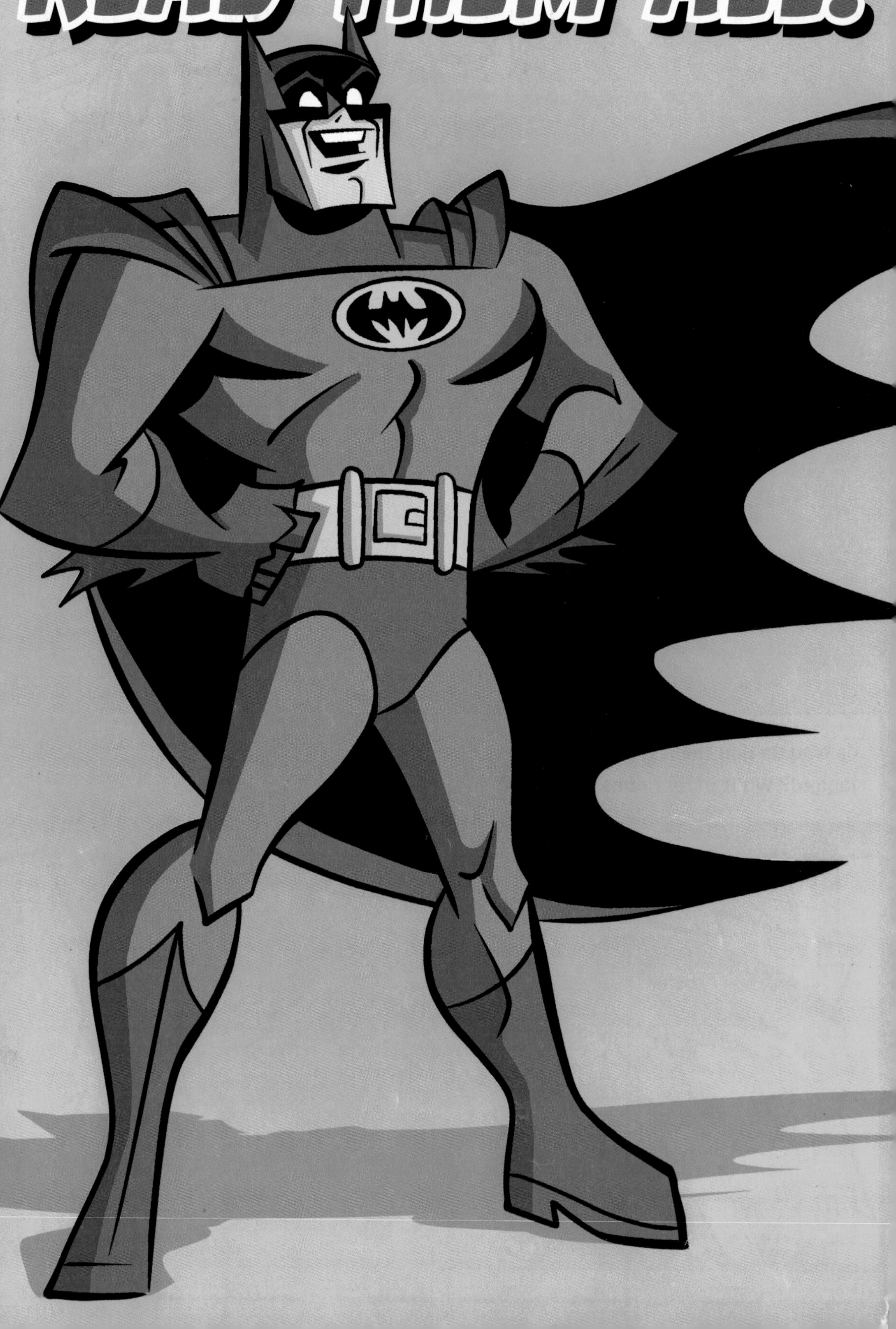

ONLY FROM...

STONE ARCH BOOKS™
a capstone imprint   www.capstonepub.com

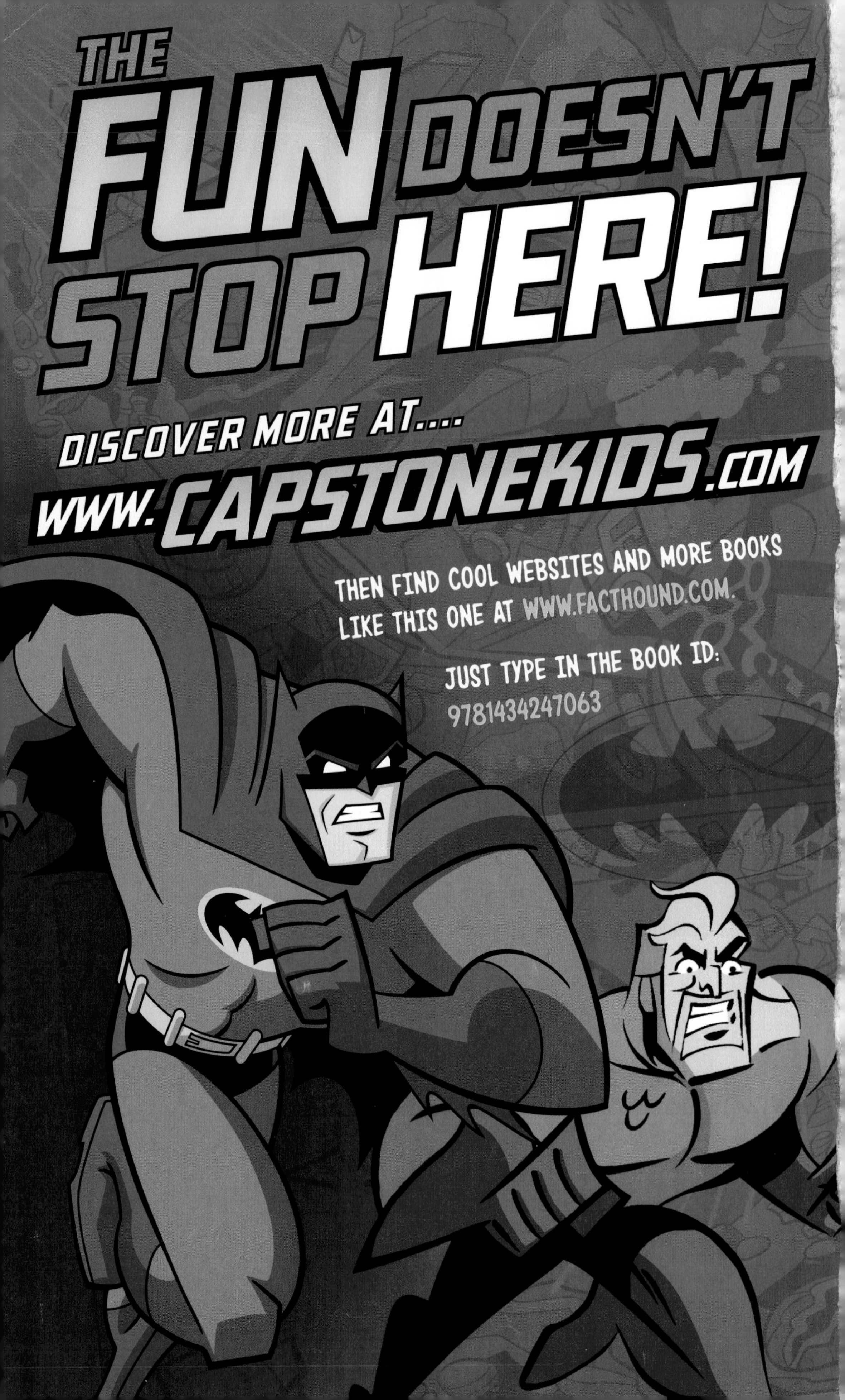
THE FUN DOESN'T STOP HERE!
DISCOVER MORE AT....
WWW.CAPSTONEKIDS.COM
THEN FIND COOL WEBSITES AND MORE BOOKS LIKE THIS ONE AT WWW.FACTHOUND.COM.
JUST TYPE IN THE BOOK ID:
9781434247063